"I'm staying for three days, not three weeks, Yannis."

"But you *are* staying," he pointed out smugly.

"Under duress. And only for three days."

"Three days is long enough to convince you to stay." Then his smile fell. He tilted his head. "Would you believe any apology?"

"No."

"Then I shall save my breath for when you do believe it."

"Save it but don't hold it," she advised.

The smile returned. "You would give me the kiss of life, surely?"

Before she could respond, he swept past her, his arm brushing hers, and engulfed her in a cloud of the cologne she hadn't even realized she'd been avoiding inhaling until it was too late.

Grinding her toes into her sandals, Keren closed her eyes and tried her hardest to ride out the wave of longing ripping through her.

They were just echoes of the past. Memories.

Memories she'd locked away on her flight out of Agon.

Michelle Smart's love affair with books started when she was a baby and would cuddle them in her cot. A voracious reader of all genres, she found her love of romance established when she stumbled across her first Harlequin book at the age of twelve. She's been reading them—and writing them—ever since. Michelle lives in Northamptonshire, England, with her husband and two young Smarties.

Books by Michelle Smart

Harlequin Presents

Billion-Dollar Mediterranean Brides

The Forbidden Innocent's Bodyguard
The Secret Behind the Greek's Return

The Delgado Inheritance

The Billionaire's Cinderella Contract
The Cost of Claiming His Heir

The Sicilian Marriage Pact

A Baby to Bind His Innocent

Christmas with a Billionaire

Unwrapped by Her Italian Boss

Visit the Author Profile page
at Harlequin.com for more titles.

Michelle Smart

STRANDED WITH HER GREEK HUSBAND

Recycling programs
for this product may
not exist in your area.

ISBN-13: 978-1-335-56924-0

Stranded with Her Greek Husband

Copyright © 2021 by Michelle Smart

This edition published by arrangement with Harlequin Books S.A.

For questions and comments about the quality of this book,
please contact us at CustomerService@Harlequin.com.

Harlequin Enterprises ULC
22 Adelaide St. West, 40th Floor
Toronto, Ontario M5H 4E3, Canada
www.Harlequin.com

Printed in U.S.A.

STRANDED WITH HER GREEK HUSBAND

To my always-fabulous editor, Nicola Caws.
Thank you for all your faith and encouragement.
xxx

CHAPTER ONE

THE CALM AEGEAN WATERS that Keren Burridge was sailing her thirty-four-foot cutter *The Sophia* through were in complete contrast to the tempest happening beneath her skin. The storm inside her had been growing since the island of Agon appeared on the horizon.

Habit had her release the tiller to grab her sunscreen and smear her face and as much of her body with it as she could reach. She'd suffered sunburn in Bermuda, a painful enough experience for her to ensure she always had a month's supply of sunscreen on board. In this respect, Keren was a quick learner. She only needed to suffer pain once for her to do anything to stop it afflicting her a second time.

Pain was coming her way today though. It was unavoidable.

A breeze swirled around her and caught the sails. *The Sophia* responded by increasing its speed. The beats of Keren's heart increased with it.

Familiar landmarks came into clearer focus. There was Agon's royal palace. There were the ruins of a once majestic temple dating back three millenia. Landmarks she'd once visited and explored at a time when she'd believed this island would be her home for ever.

The imposing crisp white villa set back in the cove she was steering towards came into clearer focus too. The rising sun danced over it, making it gleam enticingly. Fraudulently.

There was nothing enticing about it. If she could spend the rest of her life never setting eyes on that villa again then she would spend her life content, but choices made in grief were choices you lived with for the rest of your life.

The left side of the cove, a sheer circular wall of rock, had a small, seemingly natural jetty. She recognised the yacht already moored there. It was slightly larger than her cutter and used purely for the purpose of transporting its owner to his superyacht moored in Agon's main marina.

Once she'd sailed into her mooring space and secured her boat, Keren clipped her mini grab-bag around her waist then carefully snipped the base of the pink lilies she'd been lovingly growing in pots.

Holding the lilies, she stepped barefoot onto the jetty.

It was time.

The jetty merged onto a pristine white beach as beautiful as any beach her fifteen months as a sea-wanderer had taken her. Fine, warm sand sank between her toes as she treaded through it to the gently inclining pebbled steps that led up to the villa. The closer she got to the steps, the heavier the weight of her legs and the heavier the weight in her chest.

At the top of the steps was a wide metal gate connecting a high wall designed to keep intruders out.

The gate opened automatically for her, just as she knew it would. Every move she'd made since sailing into the cove had been watched by an army of security cameras. The faceless people watching them knew to admit her at any time without question or intrusion. Yannis had kept his word on that score, if nothing else.

The villa's grounds were vast and immaculately maintained. She followed the path that snaked the swimming pool and entertaining space, refusing to let memories pierce her or slow her pace.

The peach tree was in a secluded part of the grounds, the only area not under surveillance. It had grown a lot in the almost two years since they'd planted it and was now old enough to bear fruit. The masses of fruit on it were beginning to ripen. Close to the foot of its trunk sat a granite headstone carved in the shape of an angel. The words *Sophia Filipidis* were engraved into it in English and Greek. It was to the side of this headstone that Keren sank to her knees.

Fresh flowers had recently been placed in the headstone's vase. She added the lilies to it then bowed her head and whispered a prayer for her daughter's soul. And then she talked to her. Told her the places she'd been. The people she'd met. The flowers she'd sniffed. The new foods she'd tried. Talking to her here came so naturally even though Sophia experienced everything with her from the wide space in Keren's heart she occupied.

When she'd finished talking, she looked again at the peach tree. They'd chosen it together. In Chinese culture, the peach tree is considered the tree of life, the peaches a symbol of immortality. Their daughter had never taken a breath of her own but in this tree her memory would live on.

'I knew you would come today.'

Her bruised heart thumped and she closed her eyes.

Keren hadn't seen her estranged husband in eighteen months. Their only communications came via their lawyers.

If he'd approached her on any of her other visits here, she would have reminded him of their agreement, reminded him of his promise to let her come here whenever she wanted to mourn in peace and solitude.

Taking a long, deep breath, she got to her feet then turned her face to him.

'Hello, Yannis.'

Startlingly blue eyes met hers. Her heart thumped again. Expanded and rose up her throat.

His broad shoulders rose and fell heavily, a gesture that lanced her chest, and then he stepped forward to stand beside her.

They stood in silence until she felt a flash of warm pressure on her hand, and she stretched her fingers so he could lace his through them and, for that brief moment, unify their grief.

It was the first touch they'd shared since they'd first stood at this spot and said goodbye to their child. If Sophia had survived her birth, today would have been her second birthday.

Returning the squeeze of Yannis's fingers, she then gently tugged her hand from his and hugged her arms around herself. 'How have you been?'

His head rocked forward. 'Good. You?'

'Good.'

'Good.'

More silence passed.

Conversation had once flowed so easily between them.

But that had been a long time ago.

She took a step back. 'I should get back to my boat.'

'Stay for a drink?'

Her fingers tightened on her biceps. 'I don't think that's a good idea.'

'There are things I want to talk to you about.'

'Do it through our lawyers.' Like they had done since she'd left him.

'Not everything can go through them.' He rammed his hands into his trousers and rolled his shoulders. 'Stay for a drink. Share lunch with me. Let us talk. And then I'll sign the papers.'

She turned her face sharply back to him. Keren had been waiting for three months for Yannis to sign the papers that would finalise their divorce and cast in iron the financial settlement.

'You have them here?' she asked.

'Locked in my safe.'

Could it really be that easy? One conversation and then they would finally be officially over?

Either the solemnity of the day had softened him or he'd got bored with toying with her.

In the eighteen months since she'd left him, all the magnanimous generosity Yannis had initially declared he wanted to lavish her with had been stripped away to the bare bones.

She'd accepted his initial settlement offer without countering it only for him to change his mind and halve it. And then halve it again. And again.

The chateau in Provence and the town house in Milan, the Aston Martin, the Maserati…all had been dangled before her then snatched away.

Now all that was left was a fraction of his initial settlement offer and she wouldn't care if he revoked that too.

She hadn't fought back. Not on any of it. Not even when her lawyer had begged, telling her she was settling for a fraction of what she was entitled to by law.

Keren didn't want to fight. She didn't care

if Yannis got the satisfaction of believing he'd won. She didn't care what the law said. They'd been married only fourteen months. She wanted nothing from Yannis but the right to visit their daughter's grave.

'Okay. We can talk.' She gazed at their daughter's headstone. 'But not today,' she added softly. She would not fight on a day of mourning. Today was Sophia's day.

Yannis either felt the same way or understood for he bowed his head and said, 'Stay in the cove for the night and we'll meet for breakfast on the poolside terrace.'

'Okay.'

'Do you have food on your boat or shall I have lunch and dinner brought to you?'

'I have provisions. But thank you.' Maybe he really had softened towards her. Maybe the conversation he wanted to have was a peace offering. Maybe he wanted to apologise...

A sad smile curved her lips. Yannis had never apologised for anything in his life.

He bowed his head again. 'I'll see you in the morning.'

Keren waited until he'd disappeared from view before returning to the cove.

Keren was on the deck at the stern of *The Sophia*, draining the water of her makeshift washing machine, when a figure on the beach caught her eye.

He couldn't be coming to see her, she reasoned. They'd agreed to meet in the morning.

But this was Yannis, she reminded herself. A man who'd proved his word was as stable as a chocolate teapot.

He waded into the water. She did her best to ignore his presence.

Screwing the base tap of the barrel back in place, she lifted her wet clothes out and placed them in a clean plastic basket.

Although he was a good distance from her, she felt exposed. Since she'd returned to her boat, she'd changed from the simple summer dress she'd been wearing into a yellow bikini and tiny blue sarong that she'd tied around her waist and which hardly skimmed her bottom.

Stubbornness fisted in her. She'd changed her 'that's not very suitable for where we're going, *glyko mou*' clothing too many times for Yannis in the fourteen months of their marriage.

'What are you doing?'

Why his voice made her jump when she'd been pretending not to watch him swim to within a few meters of her, she didn't know.

'Hanging my washing.'

'You have a washing machine?'

She tapped her repurposed barrel.

'That's your washing machine?'

'Yep. There's rocks in the bottom of it. Add clothes, washing powder and water and set sail. The motion of the waves makes it all act as a washing machine and my clothes come out all clean and fresh.' She didn't mean to babble. Nerves and a need to prove his second unexpected appearance that day didn't bother her in the slightest had loosened her tongue.

How could he make that puzzled look when treading water? It was a look she'd become far too familiar with and usually came about when she did something he wouldn't do or didn't understand.

'Wouldn't a washing machine be easier?'

'Doubt it. Takes too much room and uses too much electricity. Plus there's not many washing machine repairers out at sea if it breaks down.'

He didn't look convinced.

'Can I come on board?' he asked.

She took a deep breath to keep hold of her temper. 'We agreed to talk tomorrow.'

'I know but I'm curious to see how you live. I won't stay long.'

She supposed she could always push him overboard if he outstayed his unwelcome.

Smiling tightly, she threw the nearest rope ladder overboard.

He heaved himself up with supreme ease and stood on the deck, salt water dripping off him, rivulets forming over the scattering of dark hair across his hard, bronzed chest and snaking down the plane of his ripped abdomen to the band of his black swim-shorts.

Keren turned away and snatched up a T-shirt to wring overboard, doing everything she could to blot out the sight of Yannis's almost naked body. That he had a fantastic body was nothing new. She'd been married to him, for heaven's sake, had shared a bed with him almost every night from the day they'd met...

She wasn't quick enough to blot those memories before a pulse of heat zinged in her pelvis. She reflexively grabbed the railing she was leaning against.

His deep voice rang out close to her ear. Too close. 'Can I help?'

She sidestepped away. 'No. Thank you.' Jerking her head at the open hatch, she added, 'Go and explore.'

Explore and go.

'Don't you want me to dry off first?'

'It's a boat. It gets wet. Just don't sit on anything.'

He shrugged. 'It's your home.'

He disappeared inside.

Her chest loosened. Taking a moment to breathe and compose herself, she then got on with the job of hanging the wrung clothes on the line she'd fashioned.

Yannis's head appeared. 'You have an oven.'

'I do.'

He pulled an impressed face and vanished again.

His absence didn't last long. 'You have a fridge too.'

'Wow. I'd never spotted that before.'

He flashed his teeth at her and ducked down again.

Amongst the clothes that needed drying was her underwear. The thought of Yannis seeing them on a washing line shouldn't make her skin feel all prickly and her insides all squirmy. It was underwear, that was all. Everyone—well, almost everyone—wore it. It was nothing to be ashamed of.

A deeper, squirming pulse right in her core rent through her to remember all the times he'd stripped her underwear from her. Sometimes with his teeth.

It was the knowledge that Yannis would take one look at these particular items and consider them ugly and unsexy that spurred her into hanging them instead of hiding them.

Who cared what he thought? Not her. Not any more.

By the time she'd finished hanging her clothes, Yannis was still exploring. There was no good reason it was taking him so long.

'Are you done yet?' she called down through the hatch. There was no way she was going down there with Yannis sucking all the oxygen out of what was already a limited space.

'Just making us a coffee,' he called back.

She gritted her teeth and breathed deeply. She would not allow herself to get angry today. 'You said you wouldn't stay long.'

If he heard that, he did an excellent job of ignoring it. Soon, his voice carried back up the steps. 'Is instant coffee pre-sweetened?'

'No.'

'I can't find any sugar.'

'I said you could explore, not ransack the place.'

'How can I find sugar if I don't look?' he said in a reasonable voice that made her want to set the fire extinguisher on him.

'It's in the cupboard next to the fridge in a blue and white packet with *sugar* written on it… Have you ever made coffee before?' Yannis came from a family who could trace their ancestry all the way back to Agon's founding, a family considered nobility, a family who counted the Kalliakis royal family as personal friends. Yannis himself had gone to the same English boarding school as the King and his two younger brothers, albeit a few years after them. Raised in unimaginable wealth he'd reached the age of thirty-four without having to do a single domestic chore.

'It can't be that difficult.'

If Keren gritted her teeth again she'd grind them to dust, so she busied herself with opening the canopy that provided shade over the small outside table and took a seat on one of the benches.

Horrified to find her legs were shaking, she clamped her hands on her thighs and willed her fraught nerves to settle.

The rawness of Keren's grief at their daughter's graveside and the knowledge that Yannis must be feeling his grief more strongly that day, too, had softened the impact of his unexpected appearance there. There was no softening the impact of his visit to her boat. She'd thought she had a day to prepare herself for seeing him again but he'd caught her out and the impact his presence was having on her made her want to roll into a ball and shut the world out. She shouldn't feel like this. She shouldn't feel anything for him.

It's just the surprise of it all, she valiantly assured herself. After eighteen months apart, seeing him again was bound to be a shock to her system.

Everything inside her contracted when he finally appeared out of the hatch, ducked his huge frame under the washing line and joined her at the table.

He pushed a mug of coffee to her and shook his head in bemusement. 'How do you cope living in such a cramped space?'

'It's ample for my needs.' Frightened of making eye contact, frightened at the well of disparate, painful emotions building in her stomach, she turned her face slightly and let her gaze settle on the calm, clear sea.

'My tender is bigger than this.' He meant the yacht moored next to *The Sophia*. Keren's tender was a kayak. She could anchor at sea, get into her kayak and row it straight up a beach, no faffing.

Her right leg started shaking again. She crossed her ankles together in an effort to calm it. 'I prefer substance over style.'

'Do I detect a dig?'

'Unfortunately, yes, so I think it best that you drink your coffee and leave. I don't want to argue with you today.' At least she had control of her voice. That was one small crumb of comfort.

'I do not wish to argue today either, *glyko mou*.'

'Then do me a favour and drink your coffee in silence.'

He leaned back and took a sip of it. His disgust was immediate. '*Theos*, that is awful.'

She clamped her trembling hand around her mug and took a sip. The coffee was a little stronger than she liked but passable. 'It's fine.'

'It's a sacrilege to coffee.' He had another sip to convince himself of its awfulness. 'I understand now why it's called instant coffee. It is instantly awful.'

'Then why don't you go home and get one of your staff to make you a proper one?'

'Soon. Your fridge and cupboards are almost empty. What are you going to eat for your dinner?'

'Food from the storage cubby.'

'Where is that?'

'What, you mean you didn't discover all my cramped boat's secrets?'

'Shall I look again?'

'Nope. There's a storage cubby behind the stairs at the bow. Now, if you're not going to finish that, you can leave. If you are going to finish it, you can drink it now and leave.'

'You want me to leave?'

'Yes. And if you come back before the morning, *I'm* going to leave.'

'And miss our talk?'

'You're the one who wants to talk, not me.'

'If you don't talk, I won't sign the papers.'

'Do you think I care?'

An edge came into his voice. 'I thought you couldn't wait for the divorce to be finalised.'

Somehow, she managed to keep control of her own voice. 'I would prefer sooner but if it has to be later then it has to be later.'

'I can refuse to sign it for ever.'

'You can,' she agreed with a coolness that totally belied the ragged heat of emotions bubbling beneath her skin. 'But if you don't sign it, I'll still get my divorce under Agon law.'

'In ten years.'

'Eight and a half,' she corrected. 'We've already been separated eighteen months.'

They'd married on the island of Agon and spent their short married life on it and so the dissolution of their marriage was bound under its laws. The law stipulated that if one spouse refused consent to divorce then the marriage could be dissolved without it after ten years of separation.

The thought of waiting that long to be fully free of him was unbearable. Surely he wouldn't hold out that long out of spite? Surely he had nothing left to torment her with?

'And how have you found those eighteen months?'

'Ask me that tomorrow.' She got to her feet and placed a palm on the table to support the weakness in her frame. 'Please, Yannis, just go. Your being here has made me angry and I don't want to be angry today. We both need to grieve and we can't do that together.' They'd never been able to.

His features tightened. His generous mouth pulled in. The startling blue eyes held hers.

Keren braced herself but the expected barb never came. Yannis inclined his head sharply and, with an, 'I'll see you in the morning,' rose from the bench and stepped off the boat and onto the jetty.

Only when he'd disappeared from sight did she sink back onto the bench and hug herself tightly.

CHAPTER TWO

KEREN WOKE WITH the birds. Their chirpy song did little to soothe the churning that set off in her belly before she even opened her eyes.

Yannis hadn't returned to the boat. He hadn't needed to. The peace she'd found in her little home had been shattered.

After eighteen months spent resolutely shoving him out of her mind whenever he tried to crash into it, he'd smashed those barriers down without any effort whatsoever. Now, he was all she could think about.

When they'd exchanged their vows, she hadn't had a doubt in her mind that they would be together for ever.

By the time she left she'd hated him with the same strength she'd once loved him. And he'd hated her too.

'Go on, then, you selfish cow, leave.'

That parting shot, delivered as he'd thrown

her suitcases in the boot of the taxi she'd called to drive her away, haunted her.

It haunted her because his fury at her leaving had been so unexpected. The writing had been on the wall for months and Yannis could read fluently in four languages.

He'd punched a wall too. Blood had dripped from his knuckles when he'd grabbed her suitcases and marched them outside.

She supposed his fury had been that she'd ended the marriage before he could.

Because Yannis *had* been planning to end it.

Suspicious of his growing closeness to his PA, the beautiful Marla, Keren had hacked his laptop—easy, when he used a combination of her middle name, Jane, and her date of birth for all his passwords—and gone through his search history. He'd been looking at divorce sites.

Three days later, Marla had accompanied him as his official guest to a palace function.

That had been the final straw for their marriage.

Agon's press had published a photo of Yannis and Marla together at that function. Keren had believed—*still* believed—his denials that anything had happened between them but she would never forgive him the humiliation or the way he'd tried to twist it to make it her fault for not accompanying him herself.

Nothing had happened between Yannis and Marla but he'd wanted it to.

He'd long stopped wanting Keren.

In the six months from Sophia's stillbirth to Keren leaving him, he'd made not a single move on her. Perversely, while he no longer desired her, his insistence about always needing to know of her whereabouts accelerated. He'd become resentful of her job. Resentful of anything that didn't involve him.

She'd set them both free. She'd escaped the gilded cage he'd suffocated her in and released him from his vows of fidelity. He could pursue Marla and anyone else who took his fancy.

How many women had he been with since she'd left? She couldn't guess. She never checked. She would not be one of those people who cyber-stalked their exes. She went online twice a week to update her blog and respond to questions from readers. Some were chattier than others. A couple in particular responded to every post and asked interesting, thoughtful questions about life at sea and the places she'd been to.

Keren also used that online time to catch

up on emails with her parents and sister. That was the extent of her online presence.

She tried to make her emails to her family full of descriptive colour and always attached photos of the places she'd travelled to and the sites she'd visited, always hoping something would inject a spark of adventure in them. Keren's love of travelling baffled her family. Their responding emails detailed lives that had barely changed since she'd left England to explore the world four months after her eighteenth birthday. In the eight years since, her sister had had three promotions, married and bought a house in the same town as their family home.

Her family were like the zebra finches they'd kept all of Keren's life, content in their small world and frightened of what lay outside it. As a small child she'd felt sorry for the tiny finches, had been convinced they must hate their cage, large though it was. Once, when she'd been eight or nine, she'd opened the cage and living room window when no one was looking and encouraged them to fly free. One had perched on the windowsill but that was as far as any of them bothered to stretch their wings.

Keren had always felt like the human cuckoo in the Burridge nest. Where the others were content and happy in their confinement, she was the bird who looked through the bars of the cage and yearned to explore, the bird who became depressed in captivity.

By the end of her marriage to Yannis, it had felt like she was living in captivity. They had both been trapped.

Her boat had only a small mirror above the sink in the tiny windowless bathroom in which to check her appearance. She rarely looked in it but that morning, after showering and dressing in a pair of denim shorts and a bright red chiffon top, she found herself examining her face. Yannis used to call her beautiful but Keren had always thought her jaw a little too square and her nose a little too small for her to be anything but pleasant looking. She liked her eyes though. They were dark brown, almost identical to the colour of her dark chestnut hair, which she'd tied into a loose knot at the top of her neck. Her mouth was boring, neither generous nor thin, wide nor narrow.

Yannis had a beautiful mouth, generous and naturally dark in colour. Everything about him was beautiful. His blue eyes. His high cheekbones. The devilish quirk of his dark eyebrows. His thick, dark brown hair which he styled into a quiff in the morning then would invariably flop over his forehead by lunch or stand up on end from him dragging his fingers through it. His strong neck. His tall frame that magically managed to be lean and broad at the same time. Yannis was a rarity, a man whose beauty enhanced his masculinity rather than lessened it. It was a beauty that had cast her in a spell.

Spells always broke.

It was time to face him one last time.

She slowly breathed in and out three times and stepped onto the jetty.

Yannis was already out on the terrace, sheltered from the rising sun by the huge pergola entwined and covered with vibrant flowers. Keren's nostrils twitched as their delicate scent reached her airwaves. It was a scent she loved.

Dressed in a pair of baggy tan shorts and a fitted black polo shirt, he rose when he noticed her approach.

Her heart was going like the clappers.

He indicated for her to sit.

She took the seat furthest from him. In the heady days of being in love, she'd always taken the seat closest. She'd sat further and further from him with each fracture in their marriage.

'What would you like to eat?' he asked politely. The table was laid with jugs of fruit juice and water and a *briki* of coffee.

'Whatever you're having.' Food was about the only thing they had in common. Their taste buds were remarkably similar...with the exception of instant coffee, she thought, suppressing her lips' unexpected attempts to curve into a smile at his disgust.

He beckoned a member of staff she didn't recognise over and spoke in rapid Greek to him. The staff member hurried around the side of the villa to the kitchen entrance.

Yannis poured a cup of the thick coffee from the *briki* and passed it to her. She waited until it was on the table before picking it up and taking a sip.

The first time she'd tasted Yannis's coffee had been on a morning just like this, after their first night together. How shyly blissful she had felt that sunny morning. Shy because it was the first time she'd slept with a man and she'd become all tongue-tied. Blissful because it had been the most magical night of her life. She'd been too shy to ask for the sugar and milk she normally added to coffee but then she'd tasted its already sweetened perfection and developed an instant addiction to it.

'What did you want to talk about?' she asked, frightened at how easily that memory had slipped in.

She didn't want to remember the happy times. They hurt too much.

'Let us eat first. Tell me how you have been these last eighteen months.'

'I've been fine.'

He raised a mocking eyebrow. 'You make me wait until morning to ask that question and now you reply with that?'

'Life at sea suits me. That better?'

'You have seen much of the world?'

'Some.'

'You don't miss being on solid ground?'

'No.'

'You're not giving much away.'

'I agreed to discuss whatever it is you don't want to talk about through our lawyers. I didn't agree to small talk.'

'I think of it like learning to walk. Start with the small steps and build from there.'

'I already know how to walk so let's just get on with it because once breakfast is done, I'm walking back to my boat and sailing away.'

'So eager to be away from me. Does it unnerve you, being with me again?'

'Yes.'

'Why is that?'

'It just does.'

'Good. It means I still affect you.'

If he knew how deeply he still affected her his head would swell to the size of the moon.

She would never give him the satisfaction.

In less than an hour she would be gone. All she had to do was hold it together until then.

'I see your ego hasn't changed,' she observed.

'I'm still the same man you fell in love with, if that's what you mean?'

Her heart twisted painfully but she jutted her chin and pointedly said, 'And the same man I fell out of love with.'

His lips tightened almost imperceptibly but then he turned his head to the sound of approaching footsteps. Their breakfast had arrived.

Keren's stomach growled when the folded omelette was placed before her. She knew without cutting into it that it was made with cheese and olives. Her favourite. Yannis's favourite too.

How many other women had been served breakfast under this pergola since she'd left?

It was a thought that smothered the growling with nausea.

Using the side of her fork, she cut into

it. She would force this omelette down her throat. Under no circumstances would she let Yannis think she'd lost her appetite because of him.

'How are your parents?' she asked. She imagined Nina and Aristidis Filipidis danced a refined jig of joy when she left. They'd treated her with their own particular type of kindness but they hadn't approved of the marriage. An ordinary English girl raised in suburbia, descended from a long line of ordinary people and with a mind of her own was not the kind of person who usually married into the Filipidis family.

'They're doing well. They're flying to Athens this morning—they're hosting a fund-raiser tomorrow night for a specialist children's cancer hospital.'

'When will you join them?' Yannis's parents had turned their attention to philanthropy since passing the ancient family business to their two sons a decade ago. Keren gave them their due, they raised huge sums of money and awareness for the charities they favoured but it was a philanthropy that sat uncomfortably with her. The cultural divide between herself and the Filipidises had been as vast as the wealth and breeding divides.

She'd been as big a cuckoo in the Filipidis nest as she'd been in the Burridge one.

'I won't be.'

Surprised, she looked at him and found his stare already trained on her. Yannis and his brother always attended their parents' charitable dos. Always. Grandparents and other parts of the extended family attended too. It was what the Filipidises did.

He understood her expression and shrugged nonchalantly. 'They can do without my presence for one function. I have other plans.'

Her heart made a tiny rip. She put a forkful of fluffy omelette in her mouth and tried to chew the unexpected pain away.

Yannis must have plans to see a lover. Not just any lover, but one he was serious about. Serious enough that he would blow his parents off for her.

The only time he'd done that for Keren had been for a function that had taken place a month after they'd lost Sophia.

There was another tear in her heart as she wondered if that's what he wanted to talk to her about. To tell her he was remarrying. It would be expected. Yannis needed an heir. Five months after losing Sophia he had sat on their marital bed with his back to her and asked when she thought she would be ready to try for another baby. She'd had to leave the room to stop herself from throwing a vase at his head with rage, furious and heartbroken that he could ask that of her when he slept with his back to her every night.

Did he want the satisfaction of seeing her expression when he told her she'd been permanently replaced or had he managed to dredge a bit of humanity into his soul and not want her to hear it from any other source? The way he'd behaved since she'd left made her think it must be the former.

He wanted to take delight in hurting her a little bit more first and then sign the divorce papers.

She would not let him see the hurt. There shouldn't even be any hurt. She'd left him and moved on. She'd spent three months learning how to sail and then she'd set off alone on the adventure of a lifetime and thrived.

He hated that she'd thrived. She knew that. He'd expected her to come crawling back. He'd shouted that at the taxi as the driver had accelerated off the estate. *'You'll be back.'*

The great Yannis Filipidis, one of the most eligible bachelors in the Mediterranean before Keren had come on the scene, a man with a life so charmed it should have been plated in gold, had to deal with the indignity of being deserted by the wife who should be grateful for being elevated to the lofty heights of a Filipidis. His ego must have taken one heck of a battering, and she'd long suspected that as being the root of his vindictive behaviour towards her throughout the divorce proceedings.

'And your family?' he enquired with the same politeness she'd asked after his, even though he'd only met them once, at their wedding. It was the first and only time her parents and sister had left the UK. Keren had hoped the trip might act as a spark for adventure in them but travelling abroad had terrified them. Her family liked the comfort of the familiar. When she'd been growing up, the Burridges' annual holiday had been to the same Dorset cottage year after year, the activities done the same as the year before and the year before that.

'They're all well,' she said. And they were. Her family were happy and well and plodding on with their lives.

'Good.'

She ate more of her omelette aware of the atmosphere developing between them. She could feel the tension encircling them, an invisible cloud of simmering anger and resentment. And pain. Pain of a love that had soured to hate and dreams that had turned to dust.

'Why did you change your name?' he asked suddenly, his tone so much tighter than the easy drawl he'd been speaking with up to that point that Keren's eyes darted back to his face before she could stop herself.

'What are you talking about?'

'Your blog.'

The piece of omelette she'd just popped in her mouth almost stuck in her throat.

Keren's travel blog was how they'd got together. When she'd left home she'd taken nothing but a rucksack full of clothes, her phone, all the cash she'd saved since the age of twelve and a laptop—a *bon voyage* present from her terrified parents. She'd created a blog in the first hostel in the first country she'd arrived at—Thailand—and began twice-weekly updates of her adventures, posting short videos and giving light-hearted reviews of the places she visited and the activities she undertook. To her surprise, she'd soon found herself with a following. Soon, she was garnering enough clicks to earn money from it. In time, she began receiving invitations from public relations people from all over the globe.

Yannis had hated that she still ran her blog

after their marriage. Hated that there were occasions she couldn't accompany him to places and functions because she had other commitments.

'We're still legally married, Keren.'

'Not for much longer,' she whispered.

'Until I sign that document and a judge stamps it, you are still a Filipidis.'

'Actually, I can be anything I like, and if I'd been living an ordinary life I would have changed it back to Burridge, legally, the day I left you. It was only because I had better things to get on with that I didn't.'

'That didn't stop you changing it professionally.'

'I would have thought you'd be glad about that—didn't think you or your family would be happy to have the great Filipidis name sullied by a sea-wanderer.'

'Don't make it about me. Be honest, for once, and admit it was it your way of sticking two fingers up at me.'

Unable to stomach any more of the omelette and no longer caring what he would think about her rejection of food, she pushed her plate to one side and poured herself more coffee. God, her hand was shaking. Her insides were shaking too.

Her teeth were clenched so tightly together

she could barely get the words out. 'I wanted to keep my professional name when we married but you emotionally blackmailed me into throwing away the four years I'd taken building my name and my blog and take *your* name. So, yes, I claimed my name back for myself but it was nothing to do with you—it was about reclaiming *me*.'

His face contorted. If he were an animal he would be snarling. 'You make it sound like I stole your name from you.'

'You stole everything from me. From the moment your ring was on my finger, you set about changing me.'

'I did no such thing.'

'Yes, you did! You disapproved—' Cutting herself off, Keren shoved her chair back and got to her feet without any real conscious thought and with such force the chair toppled over. 'Forget it. I'm not doing this again. Tell me what you want to talk about right now or I'm off.'

His throat moved. He closed his eyes and his shoulders rose and fell as he breathed in and out deeply. By the time his gaze landed back on her, only the steel in his eyes betrayed that he was feeling anything but nonchalant. 'I want us to try again.'

CHAPTER THREE

OPEN-MOUTHED, KEREN STARED at him with a violence of emotions building deep within her, bubbling and frothing, expanding and swelling, until they exploded in a gush of agonised fury.

'You cruel, vindictive *bastard*. You went to all these lengths just to toy with me and suck me into one of your sick games?'

And she'd fallen for it. She'd given him the benefit of the doubt and met with him when she should have known he just wanted to continue his torture of her a bit longer. He was like a cat with a mouse in its paws, clawing and clawing at it but never striking the deadly blow that would put it out of its misery.

'I'm not playing a game, *glyko mou*,' he said steadily. 'I want you back.'

'Oh…just *stop*! Do you really think I'm stupid enough to fall for that? And are you really so stupidly arrogant you think I want *you* back?'

Blue eyes locked on hers, Yannis rose slowly to his feet. 'Not arrogance. Hope.'

'Don't give me that. I know the way your pathetic mind works—you've imagined me secretly pining and regretting leaving you for all this time and thought you'd say the magic words and I'd fall at your feet in gratitude and relief, and then while I'm down there, give me a good kick and finally satisfy your pathetic ego by ending our marriage on *your* terms. Are you going to sign the damned papers or not?'

Jaw clenched tightly, knuckles on the table, he leaned forward. 'Not until you get off your soapbox and *talk*.'

'Then fine! Don't sign them. Stay married to a woman you hate and who hates you and stop yourself remarrying and producing the heir you're so desperate for out of spite.'

The deep burn behind her eyes blurring her sight, Keren spun around and stormed away before he could witness the tears fall. Angry tears. Furious tears. Pouring down her cheeks like a waterfall. Blinding her. But she didn't slow her pace, not even when she lost her footing and stumbled, corrected herself and walked as fast as she could to the steps that would lead her down to the beach and to her boat and freedom.

Holding tightly to the rail, she skipped down the pebbled steps, her pace turning to a run when her feet hit the sand. She was halfway to the jetty when she realised something was wrong. Wiping more tears away, she had to blink a number of times to clear her eyes enough to see.

And when she could see, her heart juddered to a stop.

The Sophia. It was gone.

Yannis had retaken his seat and donned his shades when Keren stormed back onto the terrace. His head was tilted back in the stance of someone taking a moment of peace and contemplation.

'What have you done to my boat?' she demanded to know.

'Borrowed it.'

Having expected him to deny any knowledge, his admission momentarily struck her dumb.

'What on earth for?' she finally managed to ask.

He removed the shades and set his piercing stare on her. 'Because I suspected from your attitude yesterday that you wouldn't have an adult discussion with me.'

'You mean you wanted a contingency plan in case I didn't fall for your little con trick.'

'It was no con, but you are correct in it being a contingency plan. I had hoped to talk to you yesterday about things but respected that with it being the day it was, you didn't want to.'

'Didn't respect it enough not to come on my boat and steal the engine keys.' The seas were too calm to set sail without using the engine. 'I assume that's why you took so long exploring?'

'I came to the boat to see you and to see how you lived and to make sure your boat is safe—'

'Make sure it's *safe*?' she interrupted, freshly furious. 'Still the same controlling sexist pig, making assumptions that I would—'

'There was nothing sexist about it,' he cut in, his own tone of voice rising. 'I have spent the last eighteen months worrying that you were sailing around on a floating coffin.'

'As if you've been worrying about me!'

'You're my *wife*!' His fist slammed down on the table making the coffee cups on it clatter in their saucers.

Keren's heart clattered in her chest with them. 'I wouldn't be if you'd stopped mucking me around and signed the blasted divorce papers!'

'I don't want a damned divorce! I want us to try again. I want us to talk and see if there's a way we can make our marriage work—'

'But you *hate* me!'

A pulse throbbed at the side of his jaw below his ear. Breathing heavily, he looked her right in the eye. 'Only sometimes, *glyko mou*. Only sometimes.'

'Well, I hate you all the time.'

'You loved me once.'

It was the hoarseness in his voice that caused fresh tears to well behind her eyes. She turned her face away so he couldn't see, trying desperately to tamp down the wracking emotions inside her.

'Stealing your boat keys was a spur of the moment thing,' he said in a steadier tone. 'I didn't visit you with the intention of stealing them but when I saw them I saw an opportunity to force you to talk if force was needed and I took it.'

'I don't want to talk,' she whispered.

'I know. Since you left you have made it impossible to contact you.'

'Not for the people I wanted to remain in contact with.'

'I know that too. So I'm forcing it. You will get your boat back on Monday morning.'

'In three days? Are you mad? I'm not staying a single ruddy night here.'

'Yes, *glyko mou*, you are. Three days to talk and decide if it's worth trying again.'

'I've already decided! And you have too, so stop with this stupid game of pretence and give me back my boat!'

'No.'

'Fine, then I'm going to…' Her words trailed off as she patted her stomach and horror struck her to discover she wasn't wearing her grab-bag.

For the first time since she'd set off on the open seas alone, she'd left her boat without the nifty bit of kit she kept her passport, phone and emergency cash in.

'Going where?' Yannis asked silkily. 'The police? There is no theft between spouses in Agon. You have nothing on you but what you are wearing.' He folded his arms across his chest. The pulse in his jaw throbbed again before he visibly relaxed his stance. 'I will make a deal with you. I will sign the divorce papers right now but date them for Monday. You can keep hold of them. If by Monday you still think I'm playing games and you still want to divorce, then the signed papers will be right there in your hands to do with as you like.'

Keren followed Yannis through the bifold doors and into the villa's main entertaining room. She hadn't felt this sick since the day she'd discovered he'd been searching *divorce* on his laptop.

She was the mouse given a reprieve but who knew the final strike was close.

Yannis had wanted a divorce. Yannis had stopped making love to her. Yannis had taken his PA to a high-profile function he knew damn well the press would be in attendance at.

Yannis had dragged their divorce proceedings on in such a cruel manner that, according to her lawyer, his own lawyer had balked when he'd changed his mind and reduced the agreed financial settlement a fourth time.

Yannis had wanted her destitute. He'd wanted her to go begging to him. When that hadn't worked and she hadn't fallen into his trap—her revived blog, now titled *The Diary of a Sea-Wanderer*, had been even more successful than her first travel blog, earning her enough money to pay for her meagre needs and build a little nest for herself—his ego would have felt the blow of failure. It must have driven him mad that she'd earned enough to keep herself financially independent, that she hadn't sent a demand for him to pay her anything.

She didn't want anything from him.

And Yannis didn't want her back. He just wanted to hurt her. This was his last roll of the dice to get back at her for having the temerity to end their marriage before he could.

Keren hung back at the threshold of his study while he and the two household staff he'd rounded up to act as witnesses all signed the documents he'd retrieved from his safe.

When it was done and the staff dismissed, he handed the two identical pieces of paper to her.

Her eyes blurred to see her own signature already neatly written onto them. She'd signed them three months ago, when she'd last visited Sophia. She'd sailed to the other side of the island and anchored in the bay rather than the marina for the night, then in the morning rowed her kayak up the beach and visited her lawyer's office.

She blinked hard to focus and homed in on Yannis's signature. It was the same as she remembered. The date scrawled next to it was for the coming Monday.

In three days she would give these pieces of paper to her lawyer and then she would sail away knowing that a call would come at any time confirming a judge had rubber stamped them and that their divorce was final.

She would be free.

So why were her eyes burning again? And why were there such painful ripples in her heart?

'Shall I keep them in the safe for you?'

She swallowed and shook her head, blinking hard to keep the tears at bay. 'No.'

'The code hasn't changed. You can get them at any time.'

'And you can change the code at any time.'

'You don't trust me?'

'I'd trust the snake in the Garden of Eden more.'

The weight of his stare penetrated her skin sending tingles dancing through her.

'Then I must spend our days together rebuilding your trust,' he said slowly.

Keeping her gaze on the divorce papers, she folded them carefully then slid them into the back pocket of her shorts, kicking herself again for not clipping her grab-bag around her waist. As soon as she escaped

Yannis, she would find somewhere safe to hide them. If she was lucky, she might find somewhere to hide herself for the next three days too.

She had no idea how she was going to cope for three days with him without either killing him or losing her mind. Or both.

'Ready for lunch?' he asked into the silence.

'I'm not hungry.'

'You hardly ate any of your breakfast.'

'I wonder why that was.'

He sighed and grabbed at his hair. 'Is it such a strain to be civil to me?'

'Actually, yes.'

'Would it help if I apologised?'

She couldn't stop her stare darting to him. 'I'm staying for three days not three weeks, Yannis.'

To her surprise, a grin spread over his face. It was a heartbreaker of a smile, all lopsided and…sexy.

She quickly looked away.

Keren didn't want to see his smile and re-member how it had once been part of the Yannis Filipidis package that had seduced and charmed her from the moment she set eyes on him.

Their first meeting had been at the opening of a new contemporary art gallery at Agon's palace that Yannis and his brother had helped curate as a favour to the King. The palace had artwork and antiquities dating back millennia, but the modern King wanted to bring it more fully into the twenty-first century. Knowing their King wanted to attract a younger, hipper clientele, the PR people behind the launch reached out to Keren and invited her to attend and review. That she was no art critic and had only visited and reviewed two art galleries in all her travels—reviewing offbeat bars and restaurants and activities like elephant trekking were more her thing—didn't matter to them. It was her audience they wanted to connect with. They'd offered to pay for her flights and accommodation and promised no interference with what she published on her blog. As Agon had been on her wish list of countries to visit, she'd been thrilled to accept.

She remembered the funky feel of the gallery. The creative and delicious cocktails and canapés she'd been plied with by the eager PR team. The buzz that had permeated the air.

But mostly she remembered the incredibly tall, incredibly gorgeous man dressed in a dapper pinstriped suit propped against the wall with a bottle of lager in his hand, oblivious to the lusty stares being thrown his way because his entire focus had been on her.

Keren had come to Agon intending to stay for a long weekend. It had ended up being her home for two years.

The man whose attention she'd caught that night and married six months later was still grinning. 'But you *are* staying,' he pointed out smugly.

'Under duress. And only for three days.'

'Three days is long enough to convince you to stay.' Then the smile fell. He tilted his head. 'Would you believe any apology?'

'No.'

'Then I shall save my breath for when you do believe it.'

'Save it but don't hold it,' she advised.

The smile returned. 'You would give me the kiss of life, surely?'

Before she could respond, he swept past her, his arm brushing hers, and engulfed her in a cloud of the cologne she hadn't even realised she'd been avoiding inhaling until it was too late.

Grinding her toes into her sandals, Keren closed her eyes and tried her hardest to ride out the wave of longing ripping through her.

They were just echoes of the past. Memories.

Memories she'd locked away on her flight out of Agon.

'Where have you been hiding?'

Keren, bottle of water at her lips, ready for her first mouthful, hid the clatter of her heart at Yannis's appearance with an eye-roll.

When she'd left Yannis's study, she'd deliberately gone to the kitchen rather than follow him back out onto the poolside terrace as he'd assumed she would do.

The chef was the same from her days there and, after a wide-eyed greeting of disbelief followed by a tight embrace, had become all tense and awkward when Keren asked if there was anything prepared that she could take for her lunch. In the end, she'd rifled through the fridges until she'd found the evening's dessert—a huge bowl of chocolate mousse. Yannis was a chocaholic. He swam a hundred laps of the pool a day and said fifty of those were to work off his chocolate consumption.

If he could steal her boat she could steal his chocolate.

'As Yannis and I are still married, I'm still mistress of this villa,' she'd said to the anxious chef with a bright smile. 'Feel free to remind him of that if I forget to tell him first.'

She'd swiped a stray spoon on her way out, then carried the bowl all the way to the olive grove and demolished the lot of it in one sitting.

The chocolatey sweetness had soothed her frayed nerves and, breathing much easier than she had since waking, she'd meandered around searching for rocks, and built herself a little nest which she buried their divorce papers under, making sure to first wrap it in the plastic food bag she'd also helped herself to in the kitchen.

If she hadn't been so thirsty, she would still be in the olive grove happily avoiding him. She'd made it to the outside bar by the swimming pool less than a minute ago and already he'd found her. It had taken a fraction of that time for her heart to set off into overdrive.

He'd removed his polo shirt. His glorious chest was bare and, Keren being over a foot shorter than him, right in her line of sight.

Leaning her back against the bar, she went for the lesser of two evils and rested her eyes on his face. 'If I told you that, you'd know where to find me next time.'

He stepped closer to her, eyes glinting. 'Ah, so you're planning to spend the time we've agreed to spend talking hiding.'

Her right leg was shaking again, and she

ground her toes into her sandals as hard as she could and dropped her stare to the strong column of his throat thinking that would be a safe place to rest her gaze but staring at it evoked something in her and filled her mouth with the remembered musky taste of his skin.

'I didn't agree to talks but other than that, bingo,' she said, then drank her entire bottle of water in one go, hoping the cold liquid would kill the memory of his taste and douse the flickers of awareness building through her.

Yannis raised a quirky brow then his eyes narrowed as he clocked the empty bowl with only a few chocolate streaks to show what had originally been in it that she'd placed on the bar. His arm stretched and almost touched her as he picked it up. 'You ate all this?'

Her senses engulfed anew with his scent, Keren could only wipe the residue of water from her lips and nod.

'You didn't save me any?'

She shook her head, screaming at herself to pull herself together.

He put the bowl back and stared down at her with an adopted woebegone expression. But the glint in his eyes was stronger, filling her with memories of all the times she'd seen that glint before. 'You really do hate me.'

'Told you,' she croaked.

'That was for our dessert tonight.'

She swallowed before speaking this time, and her words came out clearer. Stronger. 'You'll have to take my word for it that it was delicious.'

The glint only deepened. 'And you'll have to make it up to me.'

'Or you could just order whoever you got to nick my boat to bring it back. All your desserts will be safe then.'

This time he raised both brows. 'You would sabotage food?'

She bit her cheeks to stop the giggle that wanted to fly out.

Yannis had a sense of humour. Like his sexy smile, gorgeous face and fabulous body it was part of the Yannis package that had reeled her in like a trusting kipper.

He'd had the power to make her laugh and orgasm in tandem, and suddenly she was slapped with the memory of a time she'd paraded around in a sheer sarong with nothing underneath and when he'd tried to grab her, she'd run off, laughing at him, goading him to catch her. This was the place he'd caught her. This was the bar he'd lifted her onto and buried himself deep inside her while laughter was still alive on her tongue.

She tried to push the memory away, but it was too late to stop the burn deep in her pelvis the memory evoked, and it was all she could do to stop herself from squirming and giving herself away.

'If you won't bring my boat back, maybe think about putting a padlock on the kitchen doors. Who knows what will take my fancy next?' she said, relieved she was able to keep her tone light and airy.

'Has anyone taken your fancy on your travels?' he asked.

All her relief and the amusement it had been entwined with were cut stone dead. 'That is none of your business.'

He leaned his face closer to hers and, without a hint of humour, said, 'It is, *glyko mou*. You're my wife.'

He was so close his warm breath whispered against her skin.

She had nowhere to step back to. By backing herself against the bar, she'd effectively trapped herself.

Eyeballing him, she summoned all the strength and rationality she had left. 'Only on paper. And being your wife does not make me your possession.'

'Not my possession, no, but you will always belong to me.'

'Does Marla know you think that?' The PA's name left her lips before she was aware she was even going to utter it.

He reared back.

'Are you still with her?' she asked, snatching at the chance to goad him into backing off some more even though the vocalisation of that woman's name...

Keren had forgotten the power that name had to hurt her, like a burning knife being slashed through her heart.

'Nothing happened between me and Marla,' he bit back. 'I already told you that.'

'I'm on about *after* I left,' she clarified, wagging a finger at him. She had to keep talking and goading. She had to. Emotions that had nothing to do with desire were swelling inside her again and she feared the moment she stopped, the tears would fall. 'I do hope you're not still with her or with anyone else for that matter. Obviously, I know stealing my boat and forcing me to stay here is all one big malicious jest for you but, personally, I would hate to think my lover was playing games with *his* estranged wife or—'

A flash of rage contorted his handsome features at the same moment his arm wrapped around her waist and pulled her off her feet and onto her tiptoes to crush her against the solidity of his hard chest, her words dissolving into the firm contours of Yannis's mouth.

CHAPTER FOUR

YANNIS'S KISS WAS HARD. Brutal. And Keren's response was equally savage. Her hand grabbed his shoulder and her lips parted as their mouths fused in a heated clash of angry passion that deepened and darkened until their arms were tightly wound around each other and their bodies were pressed so tightly nothing could prise them apart.

Maybe, if the recent lancing memory of their laughter-filled frantic coupling at this very spot wasn't so fresh in her mind, Keren would have remained lost in the headiness of a desire that had sprung from nothing to something in the blink of an eye, but when she was lifted entirely off her feet and sat on the bar, panic replaced the hunger and she wrenched her face away and pushed at his chest.

'Get off me!'

He released her immediately and stepped

back. He stared at her, breathing heavily, jaw tight, not blinking.

Terrified that her words didn't match the heated feelings rampaging through her, she slid off the bar and, legs too jellified to run, staggered to the side of the pool and threw herself in.

Submerged, the effect of the chill of the water on her sun-soaked skin was immediate. It doused the flames of Yannis's kisses and sharpened her mind.

She'd fallen for another of his traps. She'd kissed him back. She'd betrayed herself and handed him a weapon she knew he wouldn't hesitate to use again.

It had been so long since they'd been intimate that her poor body had reacted like a moth to a flame.

How many nights had she lain awake willing him to roll over and make love to her?

How many times had she pressed herself against his back and slipped an arm around his waist only for his hand to clamp onto hers and stop any roaming? Sometimes he would bring her hand to his mouth and kiss it but more often than not he would lace his fingers through hers and fall asleep without a word.

In the end, she'd stopped trying. A woman

could only take rejection so many times before she protected herself from it.

The glue that had bound them together had dissolved.

And then they'd dissolved.

And now he had the nerve to kiss her like his desire for her had never died.

Or had it been so long that she'd become a novelty to him again?

The sharpening of her mind dulled at the edges the moment she broke the surface and found him at the water's edge looking down at her and another rush of longing ripped through her.

Turning from his stare, she kicked her legs and swam the length of the professional-size pool. When she reached the end, she climbed up the steps then stepped on the grass and laid with a flump on her back.

Eyes closed, her heart thumped so hard it was difficult to breathe but she put all her focus on it, inhaling deeply, exhaling, in and out, in and out.

She had no idea how long it took for her heart to steady into a mere erratic shudder of beats.

She could still feel Yannis's mouth against hers.

A shadow fell over her.

Her heart careered back into a canter.

Keeping her eyes shut, she whispered, 'Go away.'

The movement of air around her told her Yannis was ignoring her order and had sat beside her.

'I really do affect you still,' he said.

Hating that she couldn't deny it without proving herself a liar, Keren clamped her lips together. She couldn't decide if his tone was smug, triumphant or relieved.

He gave a low rumble of laughter. 'You're not denying it.'

'You forced yourself on me,' she said with as much coldness as she could inject.

'Look at my shoulder and tell me who did the forcing.'

She opened her eyes to find Yannis's face hovering over hers.

He gave a knowing smile and pointed a finger to a bronzed shoulder with vivid red lines on it. Scratches. Made by her nails.

Mortified, she closed her eyes again. 'Sorry,' she muttered.

'I'm not. I've missed receiving your war wounds.'

She scrambled up and hugged her knees to her chest, bitterness filling her to hear such a lie, colour flaming over her cheeks to know his burst of passion towards her was a lie too. 'If you kiss me again, I'll bite your tongue.'

'Kinky.'

'This isn't a joke, Yannis. We're not together any more and you—'

'Yes, we are.'

'No, we're—'

'We're legally husband and wife.'

'Not for much longer.'

'But I still have time. I am prepared to do anything to convince you to destroy those papers and come home for good.'

She pulled her soggy sandals off. 'How many times do I have to tell you that I'm not coming home?'

'And how many times do I have to tell you that I'm going to change your mind? You loved me once, *glyko mou*. We were happy.'

'That happiness didn't last long.'

'But you admit we *were* happy once,' he said, pouncing on that admission. 'There is nothing to stop us being happy again, and I have already proved that I still affect you…' His eyes sparkled before he bowed his head and pressed a kiss to her bare knee.

Before she could react, Yannis jumped to his feet and grinned. 'I have all the tools I need and three days with you as my captive to make you see our marriage deserves a second chance.'

'So you admit I'm your captive?'

His grin widened. 'Trust me—I'm a very generous captor.'

'Where are you going?' she shouted as he bounded away.

He turned and, walking backwards, said, 'Missing me already?'

She scowled.

He laughed. 'Wait there. I will be back in five minutes. Don't try to hide from me again, *glyko mou*… Not unless you *want* to be caught…'

Yannis returned carrying a pitcher of fruit cocktail and two glasses and with a blanket slung over his shoulder.

Placing the drinks on the floor tiles by the pool, he then spread the blanket out on the grass, reached into the back pocket of his swim-shorts and pulled out a blue bottle. 'Catch,' he said cheerfully, and lobbed it over to her.

Keren caught it with one hand. It was a bottle of sunscreen.

Feeling strangely choked, she examined it, recognising it as the brand and factor she'd always used when she lived here. She'd never realised Yannis had noticed.

He must have gone out of his way to buy it for her... Okay, get a member of staff to buy it for her. But the idea would have come from him.

She should be angry that he'd been so certain he'd be able to trap her here, not touched that he'd thought of such a small thing for her.

'Thank you,' she whispered.

A gleam flashed in his eyes. 'Do you need help putting it on?'

'No.'

'Sure? I would be more than happy to help.'

She just fixed him with a stare then squirted some of the sunscreen in her hands and smeared it over her face.

'I remember when you liked for me to cover you in that stuff.'

'Don't go there,' she warned.

'Why? Scared it will make you hot?'

'No, scared it will make me vomit.'

He laughed. 'You are such a liar.' He patted the space of the blanket next to him. 'This is more comfortable than lying on the grass.'

'My shorts are wet. I've got nothing to change into,' she added accusingly, only just realising. 'I'm going to be stuck in these things all weekend.'

'My wardrobe is at your disposal…just as it always was.'

She turned her face from him and wished she had her sunglasses. Yannis was too good at reading her. He was good at everything. But reading her, he was a pro. And she hated that. At least her sunglasses would give her a shield to hide behind and then he wouldn't be able to see the pain that lanced her whenever he casually referred to a time when they had been happy. Happy enough for Keren to steal his shirts and T-shirts to roam the villa and grounds in.

'If you don't want to wear my clothes then I suppose you'll just have to wear your own,' he said with a heavy, disappointed sigh.

'My own clothes are on my boat. You know, the boat you stole.'

'But the clothes you left behind are still here.'

She turned her stare sharply back to him. 'Seriously?'

His face was unreadable. 'In your dressing room exactly where you left them.'

'Why are they still there?'

'They've been waiting for you to return.'

'I don't believe you.'

He shrugged and poured them both a glass of the fruit cocktail. 'You will be able to see for yourself. For now, come and sit on the blanket before the bugs bite your skin.'

Damn him for knowing the exact thing to say, and it was a measure of how affected she was at being here, with Yannis, in this situation, that Keren had laid herself on the grass and was still sat there with no thought of the pesky bugs she hated. But now she was thinking of them and plonked herself on the blanket but as far from him as she could get.

It wasn't far enough.

He passed a glass to her.

Taking care not to let their fingers touch, she took it from him and had a large drink.

'Wow, that's strong!' she gasped when her taste buds registered the unexpected hit of alcohol.

He grinned. 'I thought you needed something to loosen you up.'

'Returning my boat would do that far more effectively.'

The look in his eyes liquidised her bones. 'The next time you mention having your boat returned, I'm going to kiss you.'

'I've already told you—kiss me again and I'll bite your tongue.'

He stretched his huge form out and propped himself on an elbow facing her. 'I will. I will kiss you…' Eyes not leaving her face, he pressed his index finger against his lips then gently placed it to her mouth. '… like this.'

His touch was feather-light, but it was enough to send sensation dancing over her skin and turn her liquidised bones into lava.

'Yannis…' Her breath caught in her throat.

A glint came into his stare as he moved his finger from her mouth and kissed it back against his own lips.

Keren was helpless to stop the tremor that shot through her, and when his gaze drifted down to her breasts she was suddenly certain her breathy voice wasn't the only giveaway of the effect he was having on her.

His eyes flickered back to her face.

'Did you ever think how well our mouths fit together?' he murmured.

'No,' she lied.

'I did. Many times. And the next time they fit together you will be the one to start it.'

'Keep dreaming.'

'I never stopped dreaming of you, *glyko mou*, and now you are here, just like in my dreams.' His face moved an inch closer to her. 'You are here with me so stop fighting and relax.'

Impossible. 'I can't relax around you.'

'I can give you a massage if that would help?'

She swallowed the moisture that filled her mouth at the mere suggestion.

If Yannis touched her again she feared it would be more than just her bones liquidising.

How could her desire for him still exist? Not just exist but be so strong?

It should be dead. She'd thought it was dead. Thought all her feelings for him were dead.

'Oh…pack it in,' she muttered.

He grinned.

Keren found her lips curving in return and turned away. Seeing him smile, feeling her defences lower while the effects of his kiss and now the light touch of his finger still thrummed through her, and her skin and her lips still tingled…

She needed to escape him. But there was nowhere to go. He would take it as a challenge.

Not unless you want *to be caught…*

He'd remembered that time she'd enticed him into chasing her around the pool too. She was certain of it. And now she remembered all the other times she'd challenged and goaded him. How she'd quivered with excitement and desire when he'd stalked towards her like a panther ready to devour its prey.

There had been times, too, when she'd been the panther.

Hunter or prey, the end result had always been the same. Ecstasy.

'I don't suppose you've got any spare sunglasses, have you?' she asked abruptly, hugging her knees tightly to her chest, as if turning herself into a ball could compress the burning throbs deepening within her. If she couldn't escape for some space then she could engineer it for him to leave. And she did need sunglasses, so two birds, one stone. 'Only, mine are on my boat. You know, the one you stole.'

'What did I just say about your boat?'

'Nothing about me not being able to mention you stealing it.'

He leaned his face even closer to hers and gave another bone-liquidising stare. 'Next time you mention me stealing your boat…' His brow rose in sensuous promise.

Her pelvis pulsed so deeply she could barely speak through the delicious agony of it to say, 'Have you got any sunglasses or not?'

He held her stare a tantalising moment longer before jumping to his feet. 'Give me two minutes.'

Keren couldn't help herself from watching him stride back to the villa. Yannis had always been as sexy from behind as from the front and it pained her to feel the old swell in her chest at the rampant masculinity of his form.

And it pained her to see him being like this, like the Yannis she'd fallen in love with. A man with a buoyant energy and a ready gleam in his eye, a man who always, *always*, concerned himself with her needs. And her pleasure.

She had another large drink of the cocktail and closed her eyes as she swallowed.

When had she lost that man?

The fault lines in their marriage had been gradual. Keren had discovered she was pregnant a month after their honeymoon and the excitement of it all had papered over her disquiet at Yannis's growing possessiveness. It was a trait that exploded after they'd lost Sophia. He'd pulled away from her emotionally but his possessiveness had mushroomed. He'd wanted to control her.

For all that, she never would have believed the fun, charming man who'd swept her off her feet and sworn to love her for ever would turn into a merciless, vindictive bastard. And now he was being merciless in his pretence of wanting her back.

By the time he returned she'd finished

her first glass of cocktail but any looseness she might have gained from the alcohol in it tightened again when he sat next to her and handed over the sunglasses.

They were her old ones.

Heart thumping, she looked from them to him.

Had he really kept her stuff here? She'd assumed he was making a joke at her expense and that when she finally looked in her old dressing room, she'd find shrouds or something in there.

She needed to look.

Clambering to her feet, she said, 'My stuff's still in my dressing room?'

'Yes.'

'I want to see.'

'This is your home, *glyko mou*. You don't need my permission to go in.'

Finding herself trapped in his stare, finding her heart swelling, she wrenched her gaze from him and set off to the beautiful villa that had started out as her home but morphed into a cage.

Keren's grip tightened on the banister when she reached the top of the stairs.

She took a deep breath and chided herself

for being a big baby and letting a surge of memories make her hesitant.

Good memories. Bad memories. Heart-breaking memories.

Their bedroom was at the end of the wide corridor to the left of the stairs. To reach it, she had to pass the room they'd had deco-rated a muted yet vibrant yellow. Keren had spent three whole days hand-painting tropi-cal flowers from countries she'd been excited to one day explore with their child onto the walls. Yannis had gone to an evaluation in Paris and surprised her by bringing back the most adorable newborn baby outfit and hang-ing it in the nursery wardrobe. Keren hadn't wanted to know the sex of their baby—she'd wanted it to be a surprise—but Yannis had known without having to ask. He'd been so certain they were having a little girl.

Placing her hand on the closed nursery door, she breathed slowly until the sharp pain in her chest lessened into an acute ache and the scream of the banshee in her head was muted.

'Do you think about her when you're at sea?' Yannis, who'd followed her up the stairs, asked quietly.

'All the time.' She took another long, slow inhalation, then continued to their bedroom and pushed the door open, not allowing hesitancy to grip her.

Nothing had changed.

The emperor bed with its hand-carved legs and matching hand-carved headboard had the same cream and mint-green bedsheets, the mint-green curtains tied back from the three sash windows were the same, as was the cream flooring. The artwork was the same. Everything the same. She could have climbed out of that bed that morning.

It was the same in the bathroom. The his-and-hers sinks. The huge double walk-in shower. The mammoth rolltop bath. Even the toiletries were the same, and she found her heart expanding as her eyes were drawn to the bottle of bubble bath.

They'd honeymooned in a private villa in the Maldives. Keren had fallen in love with the bubble bath and shower gel their bathroom had been supplied with. It smelled like pure fresh jasmine. When they'd returned home to Agon, Yannis had surprised her with a delivery of it. He'd gone out of his way to source it and import it, just for her. Every time she'd run low, he'd noticed and ordered more for her. She'd never had to ask.

A wave of sadness washed over her and

she closed her eyes to ride through it before stepping into her dressing room.

The room had a wide central walkway splitting two walls of built-in floor-to-ceiling wardrobes. She slid the first door open.

When Keren had left, she'd packed two suitcases of clothes and possessions to take with her. The rest, much of it never worn, she'd left.

The more she slid the wardrobe doors and pulled the drawers open, the more she realised it was exactly as she had left it. Exactly. Nothing had been moved.

Bewildered, she looked at Yannis, who was stood leant against a wardrobe by the door. 'Why have you kept all this?'

He folded his arms loosely around his chest. 'I told you, they've been waiting for your return.'

'I assumed you'd had a bonfire with them or something.'

A smile played on his lips. 'The thought did cross my mind on occasion.'

'So what stopped you? It's not as if you ever liked any of my clothes.'

'What are you talking about?'

'Yannis, you hated the way I dressed.'

A deep groove formed in his brow. The pulse on his jaw just below his earlobe throbbed. 'I loved the way you dressed. You always looked beautiful.'

'Every time we left the villa, you would check me over like I was some kind of prize pony about to enter its first dressage competition. You were always critical of what I wore.'

'I was never critical.'

'"*Do you not think that colour is a little gaudy for the palace,* glyko mou*?"*' she mimicked. 'If that's not a criticism then please, tell me what is.'

He stared at her for the longest time, breathing deeply. 'I was trying to help you.'

She laughed without mirth. 'Help me? Is that what you call it?'

The pulse in his jaw was going like the clappers. 'Don't you remember how upset you were when I introduced you to my parents, and my mother called your dress *interesting*?'

As if she was likely to forget that.

Keren had been incredibly nervous about meeting Yannis's parents. She'd met his brother, Andreas, and his husband, Pavlos, within days of her and Yannis getting together and they'd been friendly and welcoming, but his parents had been on a world cruise and she'd had to wait four months to meet them. By then, she and Yannis were engaged and their wedding preparations in full swing.

She'd chosen her dress for the occasion with great care. It had been vibrant red with Chinese flowers embroidered on it, a maxi-dress that actually suited her short frame.

Nina Filipidis, resplendently power-dressed from top to tail in designer fashion, had embraced her warmly enough then stepped back and, holding Keren's hands, looked her up and down. 'What an interesting dress,' she'd said in the tone of someone who'd just been presented with the most diabolical painting by a small child. Later, to add insult to injury, Nina had slipped her a business card with her personal shopper's details on it so that Keren, 'Could have some help refreshing your wardrobe.'

'You rightly interpreted that as her calling your dress horrible,' Yannis continued. 'She didn't say it to hurt you, that's just her way and it's what Agon high society as a whole is like, but you were hurt and I didn't want to see you upset like that again. That's why I occasionally commented on your choice of clothing if we were attending a high-profile function and I thought what you were wearing might raise eyebrows. I wanted you to feel comfortable in my world and that you belonged.'

'You mean you wanted me to conform in my clothing in the same way you expected me to conform with everything else in your world,' she disputed, doing her best to keep control of the emotions rising inside her.

'I never expected you to conform.' His face was so taut she could see the veins at his temples. 'I knew who I was marrying but it was my job as your husband to protect you and help you navigate my world.'

'No, it wasn't. Your job was to love and support me but you...' Something inside her snapped and she shoved the drawer she'd had her hand on the entire conversation shut. 'Oh, forget it. I'm not going to waste my breath on old arguments that never get resolved.'

This was too much. Emotions she'd believed dead were rising sickeningly fast. She needed to be away from Yannis. She needed air.

She hurried to the door, only just managing to stop before she collided into him when he stepped in front of her.

Taking a hasty step back, she gritted her teeth. 'Will you please let me pass.'

'No. Because we *are* going to have these arguments again, and this time we're going to resolve them.' To make his point, Yannis turned the key in the lock then put it in his back pocket, physically blocking her exit for good measure.

CHAPTER FIVE

KEREN SWALLOWED BACK the rising panic. 'Move away from the door, Yannis.'

'No.' He folded his arms around his chest. 'I'm not letting you run away again.'

'Let me out!'

'We're not going anywhere until we've thrashed this out.'

'You can't keep me prisoner!'

'If you want to leave, the key's in my pocket. Help yourself to it.'

'I will never touch you again,' she spat.

'Then sit down and talk to me.'

'This is ridiculous.'

'I agree. But we are still doing it. We're going to discuss all our grievances, like we should have done a long time ago.'

'If you have *grievances* against me then why in hell would you want me back? You're better off without me. You can't turn a macaw into a zebra finch. Your mother knew that from the moment she laid eyes on me. Go and get yourself a high-society Agonite bride and make everyone happy.'

'If I'd wanted an Agonite wife I would have married one and not an outsider.'

'Then why did you spend our marriage trying to change me into one?'

'I tried to help you adapt to my world. There is a big difference.'

She laughed grimly. 'Being an outsider is no big deal for me, Yannis. I've *always* been an outsider, you know that. My parents and sister have been baffled by me since I learned to talk but they still loved me and tried their best to understand me, but you just pretended to understand. You married me knowing I wouldn't be the kind of wife your family and Agon high society is used to. You told me you loved me exactly as I am but then as soon as your ring was on my finger, you tried to mould me into being an identikit high-society wife. I spent the first eighteen years of my life dreaming about the day I could break free from the straitjacket of my world and ended up with you trying to shoehorn me into a different kind of one.'

The pulse in his jaw set off again. 'Is that the excuse you tell yourself for running away from me?'

'It's not an excuse.'

'Yes, it is,' he disputed unwaveringly. 'And you know it too.'

'You are so ruddy arrogant, thinking you know my mind better than I do.'

'If it's arrogance then why are you crying?'

She'd hardly been aware of the hot tears splashing over her cheeks and, horrified to be crying in front of him, swiped them away violently. 'Because I'm *angry*.'

At least, that's what she thought it was frothing with such intensity inside her. Anger. But there was pain in there too. And fear. And the harder she tried to smother them, the harder they fought back and refused to be doused.

His chin jutted. 'Good.'

'My God, are you *trying* to make me angry?'

'I'm trying to make you open up and show some damn emotion. You bottle things up.'

'We spent the last few months of our marriage doing nothing but argue, so that was hardly bottling things up.'

'Arguing about everything but what really mattered to mask what we were really feeling. I was guilty of it too, but I'm not the one who ran away before we could resolve things.'

Fresh panic nibbled at her chest. 'You threw my suitcases in the back of the taxi! You called me a selfish cow!'

'Because I was angry, damn it!'

'Angry that I got there first, you mean. You wanted us to be over as much as I did.'

'Absolutely not. When I made our vows, I made them for life, not for fourteen months. I told you when we married, not one single Filipidis marriage has ended in divorce. Not ever.'

Sickened, remembering his search history, she shook her head in disbelief.

Yannis dragged his fingers over his face. 'You married into the Filipidis family, Keren. I didn't let you marry me blind. I did love you as you are, and I didn't want to change you, but you knew there would be expectations of you as my wife.'

Hearing his love for her in the past tense should not feel like a rip in her heart. It should not make her voice tremulous. 'Yes, to attend functions, host dinner parties, smile pleasantly and not say anything controversial.'

'Image is important to our business and to the family name,' he said, the steadiness of his tone belied by the pulse still throbbing madly on his jaw. 'You knew this. You knew this would be part of our marriage. You always knew the business would have to be a priority. It's been in the family since—'

'Time began,' she finished for him. Suddenly weary, Keren dragged her legs to the end of the room and sank onto her dressing table chair.

The Filipidises had traded in antiquities and fine art for so long the dates around the actual founding of the business were hazy. Best estimates were mid-sixteenth century, solid records established by the late sixteenth century. They had bought and sold items adorned by palaces and embassies the world over. Their monthly auctions regularly made international headlines.

'Whereas I just had a silly little blog.'

'I never called it that.'

'You thought it was insignificant.'

'In comparison, yes, and you admitted as much too but I always supported you with it.'

'Liar. You hated me running it.'

'No, *glyko mou*, I *did* support it in the beginning, as much as I could, because I knew how much it meant to you. You travelled with me on business, right from the time we got together, long before we married. You came on my overseas trips and went off exploring while I was in meetings...' He stopped mid-speech and inhaled deeply. 'But you lost interest in your blog long before you had to stop flying.'

'That's because we only ever travelled to boring cities. You promised we would see new places. I like travelling to new places, going off the beaten track, seeing things I've never seen before, new experiences…'

'We never had the chance to go to the new places I'd promised, but that wasn't why you lost interest in it,' he refuted calmly but tightly. 'You lost interest because we had something wonderful and amazing to look forward to but that something amazing and wonderful was taken from us…'

She wanted to cover her ears and scream to drown out his voice.

'…and when you started your blog up again, you did it without any consultation with me. You announced it over the dinner table, just casually mentioned you were flying to Morocco for a long weekend and then went mad when I objected.'

She swallowed hard and whispered, 'You had no right to object. You're not my lord and master. I didn't need your permission.'

'I never said you did but as your husband, I had every right to object.' He gritted his teeth and took an enormous breath. 'I never did anything without consulting you first—'

'Telling is not the same as consulting.'

'And you once consulted me over everything too,' he continued as if she hadn't just interrupted him. 'We discussed things. Like grown-ups.'

'You stopped treating me like a grown-up and started treating me like a possession. You criticised every little thing I did. You didn't want me doing anything. I *went mad* when you objected to me going to Morocco because I knew it was more than an objection. You didn't want me working.'

'You're right. I didn't.'

'I knew it! You wanted me to be a kept woman.'

'No, I wanted you home and safe.'

'Home and safe and under your thumb and under your control. Easier to watch over.'

'Yes.'

Unprepared for this admission, she stared at him. 'You *admit* it?'

His gaze didn't falter. 'Yes.'

Dumbfounded, her mind a sudden blank canvas, Keren stared at the man she'd once loved so much she'd been unable to envisage her life without him, and was scrambling for a coherent thought when the buzzer in their bedroom echoed through the dressing room door.

Yannis grimaced and closed his eyes, and muttered something that sounded like a curse. 'I need to answer that.'

Still unable to speak, she nodded.

The buzzer that had rung out was part of a system installed in every room of the villa, used only in the event of an emergency if Yannis was uncontactable by any other means. It was the communications of last resort.

He pulled the key out of his back pocket and unlocked the door. 'This conversation isn't finished,' he warned.

And then he was gone.

Alone, Keren buried her head in her hands and fought back tears. Twice today she'd cried. They'd leaked out all by themselves and she didn't know why or where they'd come from. What frightened her the most was that she'd cried in front of Yannis. She'd cried with him the day they'd lost Sophia but then the tears had dried up, sucked away and swallowed into the giant crevice of pain in her heart. So many times she had caught him watching her. It had felt almost that he was *willing* her to break down and cry. She'd been unable to.

She'd accused Yannis of wanting to police her every move many times and he'd always denied it. And now that he'd finally admitted it…

There was an irony that she'd spent the entire time Yannis had locked her in the dressing room wanting to do nothing but escape from him but now he'd left, she wanted nothing more than to drag him back and demand the answers her shattered brain had been unable to form.

She hadn't wanted any of this. She would have been happy to live the rest of her life without this conversation and without ever setting eyes on Yannis again. Why rake coals over the past and rip open old wounds just for the sake of it?

Raising her head, her eye was drawn to the beautiful fruitwood jewellery box that had pride of place on her dressing table. Yannis had bought it for her on their first wedding anniversary to home all the jewellery he'd lavished her with. Its lid was inlaid with a carving of their entwined wedding rings. On it, in the centre of the carving, were her real-life wedding and engagement rings. The last time she'd seen them had been when she'd left them on his dresser right before she'd walked out of their room for what she'd believed to be the last time.

She stared at the rings for an age before carefully picking them up and placing them in the palm of her trembling hand.

The wedding ring was a simple gold band with their initials and their wedding date delicately inscribed on the inside. Yannis had a matching one, and her heart lurched violently as she finally allowed herself to acknowledge that he still wore his, a fact she'd refused to let her mind travel to until now.

Had he kept it on for the entirety of their separation? Or had he put it back on today for effect?

Her engagement ring was an entirely different kettle of fish. It was a family heirloom, originally commissioned in the eighteenth century by Alexios Filipidis for his bride, the Agon Princess Theodora. The ring had been passed to Yannis on his paternal grandmother's death. When he'd slid the ring on Keren's finger she'd been overawed to think she was the possessor of a ring originally worn by a royal princess. She'd been overawed at the weight of history on her finger.

It had been the only moment prior to their marriage when doubt had reared its head over whether she was doing the right thing.

In that respect, Yannis was right. She *had* known what she was marrying into. An old and noble family. And she remembered, too, him telling her there had never been a Filipidis divorce.

There had never been a Burridge divorce that she was aware of either, but she'd always assumed that was because the rest of her clan were like her immediate family. Terrified of change. You married and you took the good with the bad and got on with it. But there was rarely good and bad in their lives because they thrived too much on the mundane. The same meal plan every week. Pork chops on Monday. Spag Bol—literally the most exotic meal on the menu—on Wednesdays. Sunday roast with alternating extending members of the family. One week the maternal grandparents, the next the paternal grandparents. Aunts, uncles and cousins often joined them too. It was the same pattern for Christmas. New Year's Eve was always spent at the dining table playing cards for pennies, the New Year seen in with a small glass of champagne, a kiss on each other's cheek and then bed.

Keren had spent her first New Year away from her family in Australia on Bondi Beach with a group of girls she'd befriended. She'd had the time of her life. She'd video called her family soon after midnight, remembered their slightly bemused, dazed expressions when she'd flipped the camera of her phone so they could share the experience in some small way. She'd blown them kisses goodbye knowing perfectly well that when the UK came to see the New Year in some ten hours later, that they would be enacting the same routine they always enacted and probably wondering, again, whether their youngest daughter had been switched at birth. If she didn't have her kind father's jaw and colouring and her sweet mother's nose and height, they would probably have done a DNA test to check.

If she didn't fit in with the people who'd loved and raised her, the very people who'd created her, how could she have thought she'd be able to fit in with Yannis and his family?

She'd assumed love would be enough. She'd assumed that so long as she gave Yannis all the support he needed then he would support her too. She'd never dreamed he would try to clip her wings.

He had tried to clip her wings. He *had*. He'd wanted her to give up her freedom and submit to being nothing but a high-society Agonite wife while he lived his life as he pleased.

So why was there a voice in her head telling her it was more complicated than that?

It was being here, in her marital home, causing that voice to pipe up. Being here and soaked in the memories of a marriage that had begun with such high hopes and disintegrated into nothing.

Yannis had fallen out of love with her. She'd known that even before he'd confirmed it when he'd described his love for her in the past tense.

But she was now certain that he did want her back. This wasn't an elaborate jest of revenge. He wanted her back for his pride. Yannis didn't want to go down in the annuls of history as the first Filipidis to divorce. The first Filipidis failure.

What she didn't understand was why this truth made her heart hurt so much.

Keren knocked lightly then pushed the study door open and poked her head around it. Yannis was in there talking on the phone.

His eyes locked onto hers. The strangest expression formed on his face before it fell back into its natural pose and he indicated for her to enter.

Curling onto the leather corner sofa, she waited for him to finish. Her Greek had never advanced enough for her to understand his language but she could tell by his body language that something bad had happened.

Whatever he was having to deal with, his stare didn't leave her face. And her stare didn't leave his. The beats of her heart drummed painfully in the growing expansion of her chest as she found herself flooded by memories of their lovemaking in this room. Yannis worked from home whenever he could but had always welcomed her interrupting him, would abandon whatever he was working on to pull her onto his lap and kiss her as if he hadn't seen her in months rather than a few hours.

But that had been in the days before he'd become secretive and had greeted her by immediately closing the lid of his laptop to hide whatever he was doing on it. The days before he'd lost interest in her as a woman and a lover. The days before he'd started seeing her only as his wife and possession.

Yet she remembered so vividly how it had felt in those wonderful intoxicating early days. The heat that had burned constantly through her veins. The sensitivity of her skin. The constant ache deep inside her. The incessant longing for him.

She was feeling it all in her now. The longer she looked at him, the greater her yearn to be pulled onto his lap and have his strong arms wrap around her and be crushed into the solid warmth of his body.

Was Yannis thinking of those earlier days too? Was he remembering how intoxicated they'd been with each other? Was he, at this moment, experiencing the same heavy ache of longing in his blood?

She wrapped her arms tighter around her chest and tried to will it all away. Tried to wrench her gaze away.

These feelings were supposed to be dead.

When Yannis's call was done with, he put his phone on his desk facedown and kneaded his forehead.

The urge to wrap her arms around him was almost unbearable, and she wrapped them even tighter around herself.

His stare entwined with hers again. His chest rose slowly.

She swallowed. 'What's happened?'

His lips curved into a faint smile before he gave a heavy sigh. 'Just a work problem.'

'Want to tell me about it?'

A groove appeared in his brow. 'Do you want to hear it?'

If he'd posed it as a challenge it might have been enough to cut through the weighty ache of the past and of awareness cloaking her. But there was just enough disbelief in his tone for it to not come across as challenging.

She nodded. 'Tell me.'

He leaned back in his chair and linked his fingers together. 'Have you heard of Phillipe Legarde?'

'No.'

'French billionaire? Founded the Legarde fashion house?'

'Oh, right, yes, I've heard of Legarde. Your mum wears a lot of their clothes, doesn't she?'

'Yes. Phillipe Legarde died a few years ago. His family are auctioning much of his art collection to pay for death duties.' His eyebrow quirked.

'They're cashing in on his death?' she guessed.

'They're selling what I would guess will bring in at least ten times what any death duties will be. There's a Rembrandt and two Rodins in the collection, along with nineteen other pieces. We're talking hundreds of millions. Probably more.'

Once, those kinds of numbers would have made her head explode.

'Let me guess, they're playing you off with Hoults?' Hoults was Filipidis Fine Art & Antiquities' biggest rivals.

He inclined his head. 'In one. I've been

working on this for months. We've gone through the authentication process for all the pieces, valuations…you know how it goes.'

She hesitated before nodding. Usually Yannis insisted the contracts be signed before any of this was done.

Clearly reading her mind, he grimaced. 'There have been delays with the signing of the contract. I admit, I took my eye off the ball.'

'That's not like you.'

He shrugged but his handsome features were tight. 'Jeanie Legarde, Phillipe's sister and heir, has notified us that unless we lower our commission, she'll be going to Hoults.'

'What a cow.'

His full lips loosened and he gave a short laugh. 'Almost exactly what I was thinking.'

'You're not going to agree, are you?' Yannis and his brother had never, to her knowledge, compromised on their fees. Their expertise, vast wealth of knowledge and the Filipidis reputation dating back centuries more than justified them.

'No. But Jeanie Legarde is a problem for me to discuss with Andreas and to think over. Right now, I am more interested in knowing if you joined me here because you were missing me.'

His change of subject was so sudden and provocative that it caught Keren unawares and it took her a few moments to pull a retort together.

'You wish.' She could have slapped herself for the lameness and childishness of her riposte.

His blue eyes glittered. 'Indeed I do.'

She sank deeper into the sofa wishing she could disappear inside its richly textured confines. 'I was looking for you only because I wanted to finish our conversation.'

'A change of heart, *glyko mou*?'

'Only in the respect that I'm curious as to how you can possibly think I'll ever come back to you when you openly admit that you want me under your thumb and under your control.'

The glimmer in his eyes deepened. 'You are thinking of coming back to me?'

She rolled her eyes. 'Get real.'

He leaned forward and put his elbows on the desk. 'What if I were to tell you that I never wanted you under my control—under my thumb, yes, because you certainly had me under yours. Under me...even better—but that I wanted you where I could keep an eye on you for reasons that were nothing to do with me being a control freak?'

The immediate slice of knives in her heart and the tight pull in her stomach stifled her vocal cords into a whisper. 'Then I would call you a liar.'

The glimmer had faded away. 'You wouldn't be curious what those reasons were?'

'The only vaguely reasonable excuse I can think of is a kidnap threat.'

'I would have increased our security and your bodyguard detail if that had happened.'

'That's why I called it only a vaguely reasonable excuse.'

'You know my reasons. You've always known. It's why you ran from me.'

'I left because I needed my freedom from the cage you put me in. There is no reason, no excuse in the world, to treat a fully grown woman as a rebellious child.'

The pulse on his tightened jaw was going again, the expression in his eyes slicing through her as much as his words had.

After it felt like an age had passed in thick, heavy silence, Yannis finally gave a sharp jerk of his head. 'You are right.'

She blinked. 'Sorry?'

'You are right. There is no excuse. But my reasons...' His shoulders rose. His strong throat moved.

Keren held her breath.

'I don't want to put you in a cage. I never wanted to. I just want you to come home. Where you belong.'

'I never belonged,' she refuted with a whisper.

His head tilted and he breathed heavily. 'You always belonged with me.' And then he smiled and rose gracefully to his feet. In a lighter tone, he said, 'And it is my promise to you that on Monday morning, you will believe that too.'

She closed her eyes. 'Yannis… Please… Don't. It's impossible.'

'Nothing is impossible, *glyko mou. You* taught me that.'

CHAPTER SIX

KEREN SAT WITH her feet in the swimming pool flicking her toes and watching the ripples they made. Yannis had needed to call his brother and tell him the news about the Legardes, so she'd grabbed the opportunity to escape him for a short while and left him to it.

All she'd done in that short while was think about him.

The sun was losing its brilliance. Afternoon was blurring with evening and her emotions were blurring with them. In one short day, the certainties she'd carried for so long had become muddled. Confused.

Footsteps sounded on the terrace. She didn't need to turn her head to know it was Yannis. The racing of her pulse told her. That was one certainty that wasn't muddled or blurred: her all-consuming awareness of him.

His shadow fell on her. 'I have run you a bath.'

She turned her face up to him. 'You have?'

That was another of the small things he'd liked to do for her before things had turned to dust between them. Run her evening bath.

His lips tugged at the corners and he extended a hand to her. 'I have to earn my gold stars where I can.'

Lifting her feet out of the pool she twisted round, then hesitated before raising her hand to his. The thuds of her heart were so strong the echoes vibrated through her bones.

When he wrapped his fingers around hers, warmth suffused her already sun-kissed skin, and then she was being gently helped to her feet.

Upright, she found herself trapped in a stare filled with so many emotions that, for the beat of a moment, a spasm of pain slashed through her at what she found in it.

And then he blinked and the moment was gone.

Mouth curving, Yannis bowed his head and kissed the back of her hand. The connection of his lips to her skin was fleeting but the heat that flooded her was as strong and as immediate as when he'd kissed her mouth.

And then he released her hand.

Keren fell into step with him and, unthinking, traced her fingers over the burning mark his lips had made. Huge butterflies were flapping their wings in her stomach and it was taking everything she had to move one foot in front of the other.

'How did it go with Andreas?' she asked as they walked into the villa.

'Better than it would have gone if he'd been the one to screw up.'

She smiled. Andreas had a much calmer nature than Yannis. Where Yannis was the fire in the business, Andreas was the soothing balm. Despite their differences, or maybe because of them, they were as close as brothers could be and both utterly dedicated to the business.

'Have you decided on an action plan?'

'Jeanie is attending our parents' function tomorrow night. Andreas is going to speak to her then.'

'And if that doesn't work?' Andreas took care of the art side of the business, was the one to arrange authenticity of their pieces and deal with valuations and catalogues. Yannis dealt with the clients and the pure business aspects: the contracts, shipping and finances. Dealing with a client in this kind of situation—although this specific situation was not one Keren had known of before—was something the brothers usually handled together with a combination of charm offensive and the arrogant certainty that their firm was undisputedly the best.

Yannis stopped walking. They'd reached the bottom of the stairs.

His smile was faint but his eyes gleamed as he traced a finger over the rim of her ear. 'We will cross that bridge if and when we come to it but I'm not going to give it any headspace until then. You are here and my only concern this weekend is doing everything I can to convince you that here is where you want to stay. Now come—your bath will be getting cold.'

Her ear tingling, Keren followed him up the stairs with a chest that felt like a balloon had inflated in it. More emotions filled it when she stepped into their bedroom and into the sweet scent of jasmine.

Helpless to stop her eyes from falling onto him, she had to tighten every sinew in her body to stop the balloon deflating and all the emotions pouring out.

She wanted him to touch her again. She wanted to touch him.

And then she remembered the long, long months of sleeping with his back turned to her. The pain of his rejection hadn't stopped her longing. Nothing had stopped her longing for him.

The longing for him was the one thing in their marriage that had never died. Even when she'd hated him, she'd never stopped wanting him. That want, that *need*, had been as essential to her as water. To no longer feel it reciprocated from him, to feel him slipping away from her, had tasted like poison. Because that need had, for a long time, been all Keren had been capable of feeling, and Yannis hadn't been able to return it because, for him, the desire had died. She'd stopped being his lover and confidante. Pillow talk no longer existed.

But she saw that old desire now. When he looked at her, she could feel him stripping her with his eyes, and it would be so easy to take the three steps to him and wind her arms around his neck, pull herself onto her toes and kiss him, and lose herself in the magic of his lovemaking.

It was the price she would have to pay for it that frightened her.

'I'm going to get a drink. Can I get you anything?' he asked.

She swallowed and raised her chin to smile. 'No, thank you.'

He waved a hand towards the bathroom door. 'Enjoy your bath.'

When he closed the bedroom door, her mouth opened and she only just stopped herself from calling him back. She didn't even know what she would have said to him.

Taking a deep breath in an attempt to pull herself together, Keren stepped into the bathroom. For the first time she noticed her robe hung on the back of the door. She pinched it with her fingers then dipped her nose into the silk and inhaled. It smelled of nothing. It smelled as if it had been hung on this door for eighteen months waiting for her to come home.

Stop it, she chided herself. Yannis's words had clearly rooted a little too deeply. Just because he said them did not make them true.

She stripped her clothes and popped them in the laundry chute. About to step into the bath, she suddenly found herself transfixed by her naked reflection in the walled mirror.

It was the first time she'd seen herself nude in eighteen months.

Dazed, she stepped closer, hardly able to comprehend the changes that had occurred. She'd always been petite but curvy. Her curves had reduced. Her stomach and thighs were toned in a way she'd never have imagined them capable of being. Eighteen months of sailing, fifteen of which had been single-handed, had toned her up and tanned her skin to a healthy golden hue. But her face was gaunter than the tiny mirror in her boat's tiny bathroom had let her believe, and as she registered this, tears pooled into her dark brown eyes.

She closed them shut and concentrated on breathing until the moment passed, then took one last look at her reflection and mustered a smile to acknowledge that at least her breasts hadn't changed.

Stepping into the deep bath, she slowly lowered herself into the frothy scented water and sighed with pleasure. Yannis had judged the water temperature perfectly.

Baths were one of the few things she'd missed from life on land. *The Sophia*'s shower trickled water out, which had never bothered her, just made her, on occasion, wistful.

The bathroom door opened and Yannis walked in carrying a glass of white wine.

'Oi!' she shouted. Well, tried to shout. It came out more like a squeak. 'You can't just barge in.' She automatically flung her arms across her breasts and a hand to her pubis even though the bath was almost as deep with bubbles as water.

He placed the glass on the drinks' ledge beside her and leaned over. Dazzling blue eyes rested barely inches from hers. 'Of course I can.' Then he flashed the most wicked of grins, so wicked it made her bones melt and her pelvis squirm, and straightened. 'Wine for my beautiful wife.'

'I'm not… What are you doing?'

Yannis was pulling his T-shirt up his chest. He winked before tugging it over his head. 'Taking a shower.'

'But…' All the breath had been knocked out of her. 'You can't.'

'Why not?'

'I'm having a bath.'

His brows quirked devilishly. 'You want me to join you?'

'No.'

'You're sure?'

'Very sure.' She had to force her voice to sound as certain as her words because memories were flooding her of all the times they'd shared this bath. Joyous, happy memories. 'Whatever happened to privacy?'

He put his hands to the waistband of his shorts. 'If you'd wanted privacy, you would have locked the door.'

Before she could come up with the outraged denial his comment deserved, Yannis yanked his shorts down and stepped out of them with a nonchalance that took her breath away almost as much as seeing him naked for the first time in two years did.

Then, with that same nonchalance, he crossed the bathroom to the huge walk-in shower.

Water drenched his gorgeous body and now Keren found herself flooded with memories of all the times they'd showered together. Those memories were a lot headier than the bath memories. The bath had always been a more fun, sensual experience—sharing a bottle of wine, teasing each other, flicking bubbles at each other, slyly groping each other. In the shower, they had been rampant and now, awash with memories and with the man she'd made those glorious memories with studiously ignoring her as he lathered himself, the burning ache intensified. Every inch of her skin tingled with the wish that the weight of water be replaced by the weight of Yannis.

And then he looked at her and caught her staring at him.

Her throat closed as mortified heat suffused her. A different kind of heat filled her when she wrenched her stare from his face and realised he was sporting a huge erection.

Her frustration reaching fever-pitch, she

pinched her nose and slid her head and face under the water. Only when her lungs screamed at her did she come up for air.

Yannis was crouched beside the bath. A knowing smile played on his lips. 'For a moment there, I thought I was going to have to give you the kiss of life.'

Without thinking, Keren flicked bubbles and water at him.

Long fingers wrapped around her wrist. Blue eyes glittered as his face closed in on hers. 'You want to play, *glyko mou*?'

Trapped in the depths of his liquid blue eyes as much as his hold, time stretched, the ragged beats of her heart and shallow hitches of her breaths thudding dimly as the world condensed to only him.

His chest rose and fell rapidly, his eyes seeming to drink her in, his breath as his mouth closed in on hers dancing over her skin.

Her eyes closed and her tingling lips parted, anticipation of Yannis's kiss flooding her mouth with moisture and heat flooding the rest of her, but before the connection could be made, the light pressure on her wrist disappeared and a swish of cool breezed over her face and she opened her eyes to find him rising to his feet.

Securing his towel around his waist, he strode to the door and turned his head back to her with a half-smile. 'When we play, it is for you to make the first move.' Then, as he disappeared into the bedroom, called out, 'Don't forget to drink your wine.'

It took Keren another twenty minutes before she felt her legs were strong enough to take her weight, and got out of the now-cold bath. The villa's rooms were so well soundproofed that she had no way of knowing if Yannis was waiting in the bedroom. After drying, she cloaked herself in her old robe and summoned the courage to enter it.

He was on the bed, dressed in black chinos and a navy polo shirt, his back propped against the headboard, long legs stretched out, ankles hooked together, reading something on his phone.

One look was enough for her legs to weaken all over again. When he flashed his devilish grin at her, it seemed the rest of her body weakened too.

'Good timing,' he said. 'I was about to check you were still alive. Dinner will be served in thirty minutes on our terrace.'

Heart clenching at the mention of *our* terrace, Keren nodded tersely and dived into her dressing room. She made sure to lock the door behind her.

That was one of the things that had played on her mind while her skin had turned into a giant prune in the bath. The question of why she hadn't locked the bathroom door.

Had she subconsciously wanted him to join her in there?

Subconscious or not, her skin felt like it had come to life. There was a zing in her blood. Feelings, desires she hadn't felt for so long, hidden away like seeds buried deep in the earth waiting for spring to come and warm them to life.

Yannis had been spring, summer and autumn rolled into one glorious season. He'd brought the woman in her to life and bathed her world in colour and sunshine.

And then winter had come and all the flowers and colour had withered away, leaving only the thorns.

She sighed and slid one of her wardrobe doors open. It didn't matter how deeply her longing for Yannis rooted. She couldn't live through another winter again.

Earlier, when she'd looked through these wardrobes, she'd been too stunned to find her clothes still hanging where she'd left them and unnerved at Yannis's presence to look through them properly. There were many she'd never worn but an equal number that she had, and an ache twisted her heart to remember the good and bad memories she associated with them. There were some outfits she would think twice about donating to charity for fear of somehow cursing the wearer with them. But there were some—many— that made her heart sing.

Eventually she settled on a deep red boho skirt and paired it with a white Bardot top, the two together exposing an inch of her bare midriff. At her dressing table, she carefully brushed her damp hair, then opened the drawer that held her makeup. Again, nothing had been touched. Having not worn any cosmetics since she'd left Yannis, it felt strange to put the mascara wand to her lashes. The red lipgloss she'd always loved felt sticky on her lips.

She drew the line at changing her tiny diamond ear studs for anything more artful, mostly because her chest tightened too much when she put her hands on the jewellery box. Keren had always loved wearing earrings, big hooped ones being her favourite. She'd loved bracelets too. Yannis had loved to surprise her with them. In the almost two years they'd been together, she'd built a vast collection of earrings and bracelets. She'd left with only the studs she wore now, which had been an eighteenth birthday present from her parents.

She remembered opening that present knowing from the shape of it that it was jewellery and already readying herself to act as if they were just what she wanted. Her parents tried so hard to buy her gifts she would like but no matter how gently she tried to steer them in a particular direction, they always went for the gifts they thought she should like. The gifts she would like if she wasn't such a cuckoo in their nest. Gifts Diane, her sister, always gushed over.

Yannis had never needed steering. Yannis had always known exactly what she would like, right from the day they'd met. And, as she checked her reflection before leaving the dressing room, she conceded that, despite his criticisms of her outfits when they'd attended official functions, he'd never suggested that she change into something more appropriate.

Maybe, in his own clumsy way, he really had only been critical in an effort to protect her from his mother's disapproval and the pointed looks of the women who thrived in Agonite high society. Because that first meeting with his mother had upset her terribly. For four months she and Yannis had lived in a private bubble and then she'd been introduced to his parents, not as his new girlfriend but as his fiancée. He'd been honest with Keren and told her she wasn't the kind of woman his parents had wanted him to marry—she'd already guessed that anyway—and she'd been so desperate for them to approve of her that Nina's criticism had hit much harder than it would have otherwise done.

She'd held her hurt in until the drive back when she'd burst into tears in answer to Yannis's question about how she thought the evening had gone. He'd been furious, had wanted to drive straight back to his parents and confront them about it. Even though she'd calmed him down and managed to stop him doing that, looking back she thought he might have confronted them another time and without her knowledge because apart from the odd funny look, Nina never again commented on Keren's outfits.

Yannis had hated seeing her hurt.

She gritted her teeth and took a deep breath.

Not only was she softening towards him but now she was making excuses for him. Even if he'd only been critical about her clothes from a clumsy protective instinct, that didn't negate the rest of it. He'd still taken to viewing her as a personal asset rather than the flesh-and-blood woman he'd married. He'd still taken emotional solace with another.

Giving her hair one last run-through with her fingers, Keren braced herself before opening her dressing room door.

The bedroom was empty. The only sign of Yannis was the indentation of his body on their bed.

She stared at that indentation for the longest time, fighting the urge to press her hand to it and feel if it still held his warmth.

CHAPTER SEVEN

THE SCENT OF FRANGIPANI, which Keren loved almost as much as jasmine, was strong that warm summer evening as she dined with Yannis on the secluded side terrace. Unlike the poolside terrace, which was a real entertainment area of the villa, this terrace, backdropped with an abundance of scented shrubbery and with panoramic views of the Aegean, had strategically placed solar lighting and a much more intimate, romantic feel. It had been deliberately created that way. Keren and Yannis had designed it themselves in the months after they'd got together, before they'd married. An enclave only for them. No one else invited. No one else welcome.

She knew why Yannis had chosen to eat here tonight. He wanted the setting to remind her of happier, seductive times when they'd been greedy and selfish for each other.

She knew she had no right, but she fervently hoped he hadn't dined with any other women at this spot or sat with them on the double cocoon swing chair tucked away to the left of the table. Just to imagine it made her feel sick.

Doing her best to tune out the romantic music floating out from the discreetly placed speakers, she fought back the latest swell of memories the setting provoked and downed the shot of ouzo Yannis had poured her.

Starting an evening meal with a short aperitif of ouzo had been a Yannis tradition she'd enthusiastically embraced.

A meze of hot and cold food was brought out to them. Feta and tomato wedges. *Taramasalata* with pitta triangles. Stuffed peppers. Olives. Hot snacks of *keftedakia*—small meatballs—and fried potatoes drizzled with lemons. Savoury filo triangles. Stuffed vine leaves...

Every item placed before them was a firm favourite of hers. And a firm favourite of Yannis. They were the items they would feed to each other. The foods they would fight over to get the last bite. The food they would steal off each other's plates.

As with the setting, it had all been chosen deliberately by Yannis to remind her of the good times. And to seduce.

He was seducing her with every second that passed, with the blue eyes that hardly left her face, with the intimate tone of his voice, even with his clothes. She'd commented once how sexy the colour black was on him, and tonight he'd chosen a black shirt, unbuttoned at the throat, and a pair of snugly fitted black trousers that showcased his snake hips and the tight buttocks she had once so loved to squeeze.

She wished she could say his seduction wasn't working but every time she looked at him her veins heated to molten. It felt like her internal temperature had been set to a high simmer.

The only thing Yannis wasn't seducing her with was his touch. As close as they were sat at the wrought iron table designed for two, not an inch of his body made contact with hers, not so much as a brush of a finger. Instead of being thankful for this, she was having to forcibly stop her lower legs from inching forward to entwine with his like they used to do in the old days.

'Tell me how you learned to sail,' he said as he topped up their wine glasses.

It was the first stray into personal territory of their conversation that night. The first real question he'd asked about her life away from him.

'An American couple I got talking to in Barbados were kind enough to let me live on their clipper and learn the ropes.'

'Is Barbados where you went when you left?'

That there was no underlying sting in his tone gave her a semblance of confidence to nod and say, 'I was very lucky. I met Lola and Eddie my first week there. They've lived on the seas for ten years. They taught me everything I needed to know then when it was time for me to set off on my own helped me buy my boat—they made sure it was fully seaworthy, helped me get it insured and helped me find replacement parts for the things that weren't up to scratch.'

'Why didn't you go for a new boat?'

'I couldn't afford one and…'

His features tightened reflexively. Keren guessed what he was thinking. Yannis was thinking that he hadn't paid her a single cent in the eighteen months she'd been gone. He was experiencing a stab of guilt.

She supposed it was easy to be malicious to a person when they were thousands of miles away and you weren't in communication with them—less easy when the flesh-and-blood person your maliciousness had been directed at was right in front of you.

She should know. She was feeling the same. Being back with Yannis and flooded with the memories of how good things had once been between them, confronted with the flesh-and-blood man behind the monster she'd turned him into in her head...

She'd forgotten all the things she'd loved about him. All the little gestures that had proved his love more than any words could say.

God help her, she was weakening towards him in ways that had nothing to do with the desire coursing through her veins.

Her heart was softening.

Frightened at how quickly everything was turning on its head, terrified at the swelling of her softening heart, she had a quick drink of her wine and hastily added, 'In any case, I wouldn't have bought a new boat even if I'd had the money for one—older boats are better for long sea voyages. If a part breaks while I'm miles from anywhere, I need to be able to fix it myself. The old ones were built to last.'

He stared at her for the longest time as if weighing up whether she was telling him the truth. Yannis was from the school of thought that assumed the higher the price you paid for something, the higher the quality, and while that was certainly true for many things, it didn't apply to everything. It didn't apply to all boats.

His chest rose before he took a swig of his wine and his mouth relaxed into its usual sensuous form. 'So you are telling me that my wife is now an expert at boat maintenance?'

'I'm an expert at my own boat's maintenance if that counts?'

His glimmering eyes flickered down to her breasts and back up to her face. 'I would love to see you in a pair of blue overalls with a toolbox in your hands.'

'I'm impressed you know what a toolbox is,' she said, then immediately reproved herself for adopting such a teasing tone. Even her voice was softening towards him.

A quirky eyebrow rose. 'Every man takes pride in his toolbox, *glyko mou*. You are welcome to handle mine whenever you wish.'

Keren's throat ran dry at the innuendo. Crossing her legs tightly together and failing to come up with a non-smutty retort, she hastily forked a roasted red pepper into her mouth.

Smirking, Yannis helped himself to a *keft-*

edakia and, eyes smouldering, savagely bit into it.

Her skin completely overheating, she had a large drink of her crisp white wine to cool her insides.

'Are you feeling all right, *glyko mou*?' he asked with faux concern.

Finishing her wine, she nodded.

'Sure? You look a little warm from where I'm sitting.'

'It's a warm evening,' she managed to say.

He leaned forward. 'It does feel as if the heat has been turned up.' Then he grinned wickedly and plucked the stem of her empty wine glass.

'Do you always sail alone?' he asked as he pulled the wine bottle out of the ice bucket.

His ability to swerve the conversation into different directions without losing a beat was, she had to admit, impressive.

'Yes.'

'Is it not dangerous? I'm thinking of predatory men.'

'There's a whole community of sea-wanderers out there and we all look out for each other. In any case, I've been in more danger with predatory men on land than I ever could be at sea,' she retorted pointedly.

Amusement played on his mouth as he

carefully placed her wine glass back down beside her plate and let his fingers linger on it. 'So you never get frightened out at sea?'

'I never said that.' His hand was so close to hers that she had to scramble her brain to make it coherent. 'Sometimes it can be terrifying—I've been caught in a couple of squalls—but so long as I keep a cool head and follow all my procedures correctly, I'm as safe as I can be. There are other things that scare me much more.'

'Like what?'

My feelings for you. 'Spiders.'

One side of Yannis's mouth curved making her certain he saw right through her lame answer. 'You must get lonely all alone out there.'

'There's too much to do for loneliness,' she answered. 'How about you? Have you managed to do much sailing?'

Keren wanted—needed—to get the subject away from her. She didn't want to have to talk about the nights anchored at sea when the weather was calm and there was nothing to distract her, when she would find herself unwittingly thinking of Yannis and then virtually crippled with the loneliness that came from missing him. Those moments had been few and far between but when they struck, the pain of everything she'd lost smacked her afresh.

His expression became suddenly inscrutable. 'Some.'

'Where?'

He shrugged. 'Nowhere you haven't been, I'm sure.' He chewed on a fried potato, swallowed, then added, 'Remember how we used to talk about sailing the world when we retired?'

A wave of sadness washed through her. 'We had a lot of pipe dreams then.'

'They were never pipe dreams,' he refuted.

She forced brightness into her voice. 'You're a Filipidis, Yannis.'

'And?'

'And you'll follow the same path as your parents and their parents before them.'

'My parents sailed the world,' he pointed out.

'They cruised the world on an ocean liner that had more staff than guests and with a full itinerary and always knowing the day they would return home. It's a wonderful way to see the world but not if you like adventure and want to take each day as it comes and go off the beaten track.'

'That can be done on *The Amphitrite*.'

She nearly laughed, and pinched a stuffed

vine leaf with her fingers, remembering how awed she'd been the first time Yannis had taken her for a long weekend away on his yacht. She had guessed it would be magnificent but even that guess had been an understatement. A floating palace was the closest description she could come up with for it.

'Trust me, my love, your yacht is way too big and would cause way too much damage to get into the best places. It's not much smaller than the liner your parents sailed on and when you sail, you have dozens of crew. Everything is done for you. It's not the same.'

It was only when she bit into the stuffed vine that she noticed Yannis had stilled.

'What?' she said when she'd swallowed her food. 'Have I just offended you?'

There was a melancholic quality to his answering smile. 'No, *glyko mou*, you haven't offended me.'

It was his calling her by his pet endearment that made Keren realise that she'd just made an unconscious slip of the tongue and casually addressed him with her old pet endearment for him.

My love.

Oh, God, not only were her heart and thoughts and voice softening towards him, but now her words were too. This was horrendous. Terrifying.

Hugely aware of the heat enflaming her cheeks, she quickly popped the last of the stuffed vine leaf into her mouth and looked anywhere but at Yannis.

'I know what you mean,' he said.

Relieved he wasn't going to make anything more about her slip-up, she met his stare. What she found there filled the entirety of her chest.

'About me being a Filipidis.' He pulled a rueful face. 'I have always followed the same path as my parents. Andreas and I attended the same English boarding school as our father, then the same English university, then the same business shadowing programme our father followed with his father. We grew up knowing that when we had accumulated all the knowledge we needed for the business, our parents would retire and pass the mantle to us. There was never any question about doing anything else.'

'But I thought you said you'd never wanted to do anything else?' she reminded him, referring to one of their old mammoth conversations when they had been greedy to know every last thing about each other.

'I didn't, but I wonder if that's because that

weight of five hundred years of history was always part of my thinking.'

'Okay, then think of it this way—if you woke up tomorrow and the business was gone, what would you do?'

'Would I still have all my money in this scenario?'

'Let's say no. You had nothing and had to start over again.'

He raised an eyebrow in mock alarm. 'I wouldn't even have a chef?'

'Nope.'

'Then I suppose the first thing I would have to do is learn to cook.'

She sniggered at the very thought of it. 'Then once you'd stopped yourself from starving, what would you do? Imagine you had the qualifications to do anything you wanted in the whole wide world.'

He sipped slowly at his wine, his brow narrowed in thought, then shook his head. 'I cannot think of anything.'

'Nothing?'

'Nothing. I am doing what I should be doing and what I want to be doing and the only thing missing in my life is having my wife at my side.'

Having just relaxed into the conversation

for the first time since she'd joined him at the table, Keren sighed. 'Don't spoil things.'

'I'm not. I'm just pointing out that marrying you is the only path I've taken that diverges from the path set for me.'

'And even then you were following in Andreas's path,' she managed to tease lightly. Andreas had married Pavlos a year before Keren and Yannis met.

'At least he married an Agonite.'

'The goody two-shoes.'

Yannis's grin at this was infectious and Keren found her mouth pulling into a wide smile of its own.

She had missed this, she realised. Really missed it. The days when they could talk about anything, veering from serious conversation to the absurd in the breath of a sentence. She had once thought Yannis was the only person in the world tuned to the same wavelength as her. It made her heart ache to think he still might be.

'I know Andreas got there first but it must have been difficult for you to tell your parents you were marrying an outsider.' More difficult than he'd let her believe she now thought.

'I knew we were meant to be together.' Blue eyes boring into her, he leaned back in his chair. 'I wish I could make you under-

stand what it was like for me meeting you.'
He smiled but there was a tautness to it. 'My
life was great. I'd grown up with all the riches
in the world. I had the best education that
money could buy and a loving family. I had a
thriving business and a great social network.
I wanted for nothing. I've never wanted for
anything. And then I met you at the palace.
You were the sexiest creature I had ever set
eyes on, but it wasn't just your beauty that at-
tracted me. I watched you circulate and...' He
closed his eyes. 'You were like no one I had
met before. The people in my world...every-
thing is done consciously. You understand?'

Even though she had an idea of what he
meant, Keren shook her head.

His eyes snapping back on her, Yannis
rubbed the nape of his neck. 'Think of all
the functions we attended together and the
people we attended them with. The way those
people behave in public, from the clothes they
wear to the words they choose when in conversation, to the people they choose to have
those conversations with. Everything is done
with advancement in mind. People want to
climb the hierarchy. Everyone wants to be
first on a guest list. No one wants to be ex-
cluded from the in-crowd, and the result is
that everyone behaves in the same conscious

manner. I never noticed any of this until I met you.'

He leaned forward and rested his hand close to hers again. The seductive tone of his voice was becoming hypnotic.

'You were different, *glyko mou*, and it wasn't just because you dressed so much more brightly and more freely than anyone else. When you walked around that palace gallery there seemed no sense of purpose in your steps like there was with everyone else. You just wandered around studying whatever picture caught your attention, not whatever picture you thought you should be studying, and you didn't look the slightest bit awkward to be doing it with only yourself for company. You were so free, and so comfortable and happy in your skin in a way I had never seen before. I knew that to catch someone so vibrant and free would be hard and that to hold onto them would be next to impossible. I knew all that before we exchanged a single word or look. And then you looked at me and that was it for me—*you'd* caught *me.*'

Keren remembered how her flesh had prickled with the awareness that someone was watching her. Remembered turning her head and finding Yannis propped against a wall gazing at her. Remembered how their eyes had locked together and how the prickling of her flesh had intensified and spread through every part of her.

One look and that had been it for her too.

The difference was she had never stopped wanting him.

But her flesh was prickling now, tingling with a growing desperation for his touch.

If she moved her little finger an inch, it would brush against his.

Yannis wanted her to make the first move. He was waiting for it. She could no longer say with certainty that hell would have to freeze over first, not when hell burned so fiercely.

'Remember what you said earlier about me shoehorning you into a straitjacket?' he said, blue eyes ringing at her.

Spellbound, her throat too constricted to speak, she nodded.

'It was meeting you that made me see that *I* had been living in a straitjacket that had been wrapped around me since before I was born. I'd just never felt its constriction. You unlocked it for me.'

The temptation to brush her finger to his was so intense and the effects of his words on her so all-consuming that Keren had to fight with everything she had to stop herself from falling into the open trap he was laying for her.

This was what Yannis wanted. To seduce her back into his bed and back permanently into his life, seduce her with his words as well as the magnetism she'd always responded so strongly to. Make her feel special. Like she was the only woman in the world.

That had been true. Once. Before he'd stopped treating her as his lover and started treating her as his little wife and acting as her lord and master. Before he'd turned his back on her and sought emotional comfort, if not physical, from another.

But how badly she ached at the thought it could still be true and that his feelings for her were still true and that he wanted her back for *her* and not because his pride had decided he didn't want a divorce after all.

She had been so right in fleeing to Barbados when she'd left him. So right in refusing any communication other than through their lawyers. The affect Yannis had on her was as strong as the day they'd exchanged their wedding vows. It had been building inside her all day like a dormant volcano awakening.

She feared she was on the brink of it erupting.

CHAPTER EIGHT

PANIC RISING AT the tempest writhing inside her, Keren leaned over and pressed a trembling finger to the button connecting their private sanctuary to the kitchen.

Yannis's stare was shrewd and knowing. 'Feeling the need for a chaperone, *glyko mou*?'

Cheeks burning at his mind-reading abilities, she smiled tightly. 'Feeling the need for tea.'

He arched a brow. 'Tea?'

'The hot stuff we drink by the bucket in England.'

'The hot stuff you drink with a splash of milk and no sugar.'

Amazed, she shook her head. 'You have the memory of an elephant.'

He winked. 'And the trunk of one too.'

The flush that ran through her at this set her cheeks ablaze again but she never got the chance to think of a comeback for a member of staff appeared. It was another she didn't recognise.

Yannis spoke to him in their native language. The staff member's eyes flickered with alarm. Keren guessed he'd never been tasked with making a pot of tea before.

'Have you finished eating?' Yannis asked her.

'Yes, thank you.'

Their dishes and plates were cleared and then they were alone again.

Somehow, that brief interlude of company made the intimacy of the setting feel even more heightened, and Keren found herself tempted to grab the bottle of ouzo and pour herself a hefty measure to calm her nerves.

She'd had enough alcohol for one night. Any more and her inhibitions would loosen too much and she'd be vulnerable to doing something she would regret. She was close enough to the brink as it was. And Yannis knew it.

One day with him and she was coming undone.

How was she going to resist him for another two whole days?

She had to hold it together for a little while

longer, that was all. She would drink her tea and then she would go to…

Bed.

Her brain turned to heated mush.

He wouldn't expect her to share his bed, would he?

Their bed.

'What happened to all the old staff?' she asked, desperate to make their remaining conversation neutral. 'There's hardly any of them left.'

His features set again in the inscrutable expression she was coming to think meant it was a subject *he* didn't want to talk about.

Why would that be the case with his staff? Yannis had always been a good boss. His household staff were devoted to him.

After a few beats too long, he said, 'They had to go.'

'Why?'

'Come back to me and I'll tell you.'

She tried to scowl. Her lips and cheeks refused to co-operate. 'Nice try.'

'I will try for ever.'

'Then you're going to be disappointed for ever.'

He put his elbow on the table and rested his chin in his palm. Her pelvis tightened at the playful, seductive gleam in his eyes.

'Who are you trying to convince of that? You or me?'

Two members of staff appeared, one carrying a tray with her tea and a coffee for Yannis, the other carrying their dessert. It was another batch of the chocolate mousse Keren had pilfered earlier.

How many hours ago had that been?

It felt like a day had passed for each hour spent with him.

Once everything was set before them and they were, again, alone, Yannis pulled the huge crystal bowl full of chocolate deliciousness in front of him and hugged an arm around it in protective fashion. 'What are you having?'

She held her dessert bowl out and nodded pointedly at the mousse.

'I have to share?' he queried.

'Yep.'

'*You* didn't share.'

'I would have done if you'd found me.'

'No, you wouldn't.'

'Well, you didn't find me, so we'll never know.'

He shook his head in mock disappointment and took her bowl. 'A pity. If I had found you, I could have fought you for it like we used to do.'

They'd fought over chocolate mousse many times. It had always ended with them having to shower the mess they hadn't licked off each other away.

They were happy memories. Pure. Untainted. And, God help her, the heat inside her pulsed even harder.

'Just fill the bowl,' she ordered.

Keren had never been much of a chocolate lover until she'd met Yannis. His addiction to it had proved contagious. The mousse they were currently sharing was from his school days. Yannis had made sure to take the recipe with him when he'd packed his school trunk the final time. The chefs he'd employed in his own homes since had had to prove themselves by making it before the job was offered to them. Muck it up and they could forget working for him.

'Can I not fill you instead?'

'Can you stop with the innuendoes?'

'Why? Are they turning you on too much for comfort?'

If he only knew how much... 'You wish.'

'To turn you on?' He passed the now-filled dessert bowl to her. 'Always, *glyko mou.*'

'Oh… Shut up.'

He smirked and dug his spoon into what was left in the crystal bowl.

'Are you planning to eat all that?' she asked, outraged. He had at least five times as much mousse as she did.

His eyes trained on her, the heaped spoon disappeared into his sensuous mouth.

'Seriously?'

He withdrew the spoon slowly. His eyes gleamed. 'You are welcome to fight me for it.'

Her attempt at a scowl was, this time, moderately more successful than her first attempt but too quickly turned into a smile that she hid by shoving her own spoon in her mouth.

He was irrepressible. Irresistible.

Dangerous.

Keren made quick work of the rest of her portion, drank her tea then pushed her chair back. 'I'm going to bed.'

The gleam in his eyes speared straight into her core. 'An excellent idea.'

'Alone,' she said pointedly.

A single eyebrow rose. A knowing silkiness threaded into his voice. 'You are planning to hide from me again?'

The clash of their gazes intensified. The beats of her heart intensified too, a loud tattoo drumming in her ears.

Keren knew exactly what Yannis was thinking because she was thinking the same thing. The liquid in his eyes told her he knew she was thinking it too.

They were both remembering the time she'd hidden from him as one of the many sensuous games they'd loved to play. He'd searched the villa for her, just as she'd known he would. She'd been waiting for him in his dressing room. Naked. Artfully splayed on his dressing table chair.

What had followed had been so erotic and so rampant that just to remember it was to feel the residue of the pleasure inside her.

By the time they'd finished, she'd been so weak and sated Yannis had had to carry her to their bed.

The charged silence connecting them stretched and tautened until his nostrils flared and his chest rose. 'The first move is yours to make, *glyko mou*.'

And then he dipped a finger in the bowl and slowly, provocatively, sucked the mousse off it.

Keren fled inside.

Yannis walked into their marital bedroom. He kept his hand on the door once he'd closed it and observed Keren burrowed under the duvet.

A slow smile spread over his gorgeous

face. 'So you've decided to spend the night with me after all... Interesting.'

'No, I've decided to share our bed with you. I'm not going to play the games you want to play, Yannis.'

A knowing eyebrow rose. 'What games would they be?'

'You know exactly what I mean, and I mean it—I'm not playing them.'

'Whatever you say.'

'You stick to your side of the bed and I'll stick to mine.'

'Of course.' He pulled his shirt over his head.

'Can't you do that in your dressing room or the bathroom?'

'Why?'

'Because.'

He undid the button of his trousers. 'It's nothing you haven't seen before.' He pulled them down along with his underwear, past his hips. Gloriously naked, he winked and stepped out of them. 'Indeed, I seem to remember you had a good look earlier when I was showering.'

Another wink and he disappeared into the bathroom.

Furious, frustrated and who knew what else, certainly not her, Keren grabbed hold of his pillow, put it over her face and screamed into it.

Every time she thought she'd found a way to get the upper hand, Yannis trumped her.

What made it worse was being unable to deny the thrills that ravaged her every time he regained the upper hand.

She was a masochist. She must be.

What had the alternative been to sleeping in the marital bed? Hiding in one of the spare rooms and then lying on tenterhooks, waiting for him to find her? Waiting in *anticipation* because the unspoken charge that had swirled so thickly and stickily between them had let them both know that if she hid from him again, it would be an invitation.

An invitation from Keren for Yannis's seduction.

She'd dug out an old birthday present from her parents that she'd never worn—a long-sleeved, high-necked nightdress that fell to her ankles. Wearing it, she would fit right in with the prudish Victorians.

The bathroom door opened.

Even though she lay rigid and had her gaze fixed on the ceiling, she was fully aware of Yannis, magnificently naked, approaching the bed like the panther he was.

She wouldn't engage with him.

When Keren had got into bed shortly before he'd appeared in the room, she'd turned the main light off and turned his bedside light on to maximum brightness. Instead of turning it off, he climbed in beside her and dimmed it to a soft mellowness.

She clenched her jaw. She'd always loved the romance of their bedroom lighting.

Lying on his side facing her, propped up on an elbow, Yannis lifted the duvet before she had a chance to keep her half of it tightly pressed against her.

'Sexy,' he mocked.

Her jaw clenched even tighter.

'You don't think an ugly thing like that will stop me wanting you, do you, *glyko mou*?'

She would not answer. Would not engage.

'I would still want you if you were wearing an old sack, but I made you a promise. You could lie here as naked as I am and I would still resist you.'

'Can't you put some boxers on?' she snapped before she could stop herself.

'I *could*,' he mused. 'But I won't.'

She ground her teeth back together and attempted to close her eyes. Attempted. They refused to obey, too busy trying to override her will and sneak a look at Yannis. She could feel his gaze boring into her.

'Will you *please* stop looking at me?'

'But I like looking at you.'

'Will you at least turn the light off?'

'I'm happy with it being on but if you want to turn it off, be my guest.'

And have to lean over him to do it? Not a chance.

'How many other women have you shared this bed with since I've been gone?' The question, blurted out, came from nowhere. Keren hadn't even been thinking it. Not at that precise moment anyway.

But it was a question that had weighed heavily on her in some form or another all day.

It was a question that had compressed her heart in unguarded moments since she'd left him.

'Look at me and I'll tell you.'

She kept her gaze on the ceiling.

'Keren?'

Her jaw loosened and she closed her eyes.

'Look at me.'

Opening them, her heart beating fast, she slowly turned her face to him.

What she found in his stare closed her throat.

Yannis's hand rose as if to touch her before he gave a rueful smile and rested it on his pillow. Gently, he said, 'The only woman who has shared this bed with me is you.'

A swell of unexpected tears burned the back of her eyes and she closed them before fixing her gaze back to the ceiling.

'What about men?' Her voice was too shaky for it to be the sharp quip she'd intended.

'I've managed to resist bringing a man here too,' he said drily.

She managed a short inhalation of air into her cramped lungs.

She believed him. Yannis could be manipulative and ruthless and occasionally economical with the truth but he never told a barefaced lie. If he said there hadn't been another woman in this bed then there hadn't been another woman in this bed.

That didn't mean there hadn't been other women though. The villa had eleven bedrooms. Half their own lovemaking hadn't even been in a bed.

'Has there been anyone else for you?' he asked in the silence.

'No,' she whispered.

There had only ever been Yannis.

Keren had watched a film set in Thailand when she was twelve—a film that, looking back, she'd been far too young to watch—and been transfixed by the setting. The beauty of the beach featured in it. The colours. To a young suburban girl on the cusp of adolescent who'd hardly left her home town never mind her country, it had been a gateway into a world she hadn't known existed. That film had changed her life.

From that moment, she'd watched every film and television series set in foreign locales, made frequent visits to the library to stock up on reading material set in foreign climes. The books could be fiction or factual, she hadn't cared, so long as they were set anywhere or were about anything but the UK. She had *itched* to get out there and explore the world and tread the exotic beaches with her own feet and inhale different scents and immerse herself in different cultures, and to do that required money. So she had worked: a paper round at thirteen, a Saturday job in a local barber sweeping hair at fourteen, a Saturday and Sunday job in a shoe shop at sixteen. She'd also babysat at every opportunity, averaging three evenings a week. All the money she'd made, she'd saved. Her sole focus had been to save enough money to buy herself a ticket to Thailand the day she left school. As a result, boys hadn't really been on her radar, and when she'd boarded her first flight she'd been an eighteen-year-old virgin.

Once abroad, she'd made lots of friends in lots of different countries and occasionally buddied up with them but on the whole had been content following her own path. She'd liked having the freedom of waking up in one country and spontaneously deciding to move on to another. How could you be spontaneous as part of a couple when you had to consider their feelings and opinions? Safer to avoid romance in any of its forms, and so a virgin she had remained. Until she met Yannis.

He was like no one she'd ever met before, and it wasn't just because he was rich—to make her money stretch, she'd always stayed in the safest cheap accommodation she could find which no rich person would be seen dead in, so had never mixed with rich people before—and gorgeous and sexy. His humour had tickled her. His intelligence had awed her. He'd seen so much of the world. He was a man of the world. A *real* man. And she'd fallen head over heels for him.

What they'd shared had been special. She hadn't needed experience to know that. It had been wonderful. Heady. Heavenly.

And then it had all fallen apart.

Her man of the world had wanted to lock her in a cage.

He moved his face close enough for her to feel his breath against her cheek as he seductively said, 'Did you miss me too much to want anyone else?'

Gripping the duvet tightly, she gave a dismissive *pfft* in answer. Her throat wasn't capable of working with her mouth to form speech.

If she ever reached the stage where she was ready for a relationship with someone new, deep down she knew there would be no point as what she and Yannis had shared before things had imploded had been too magical for her to replicate with anyone else. There was no one in the world who compared with him.

The warmth of his breath left her face as he twisted to turn the light off, plunging the room into darkness.

Her awareness of the man lying naked beside heightened. Her heart beat even faster. Suddenly she was aware of the cotton of her nightdress pressed lightly against her increasingly sensitive skin, and she tightened her grip on the duvet to stop herself yanking it off.

'You are having trouble breathing, *glyko mou*?'

She swallowed her parched, constricted

throat. 'I'm fine,' she lied. Her lungs didn't seem to want to open. 'Go to sleep.'

'How can I sleep if I can't hear you breathe? I worry you might need the kiss of life.'

'Touch me, and I'll kick you where it hurts.'

'I love it when you talk dirty.'

She clamped her lips together. She must not indulge him. That was what he wanted. To provoke her.

He pushed his half of the duvet off and stretched. 'Is it me, or is it hot in here?'

'It's you.' The discarded half of duvet had bunched between them but the extra barrier made not the slightest bit of difference to her, not when on the other side of the barrier Yannis lay with his nakedness exposed.

'I shall turn the air conditioning up,' he decided, twisting again to do just that from the control box beside his bedside light.

'Do what you like, just go to *sleep*.'

Frustrated, both with him and herself, Keren turned her back to him.

A moment later cool air brushed her forehead and tip of her nose, the only parts of her body not cocooned in the duvet.

And then Yannis stretched back out again, except this time he rolled onto his side and inched his way behind her, positioning himself close enough that now his breath tickled then warmed the top of her head.

Trying, again, to drag air into her lungs she edged away from him. He closed the gap in an instant.

'Will you move over to your own side?' she tried to snap. It came out more like a wail.

'But your side is warmer than mine.'

'You just said you were too hot!'

'And now I am cold.'

'Then turn the air conditioning off or get back under the duvet.'

He sighed as if she were asking something that was a major imposition. 'Okay. I will go back to my side and get cold if you insist.'

'I do.'

He sighed again and shuffled away from her.

Her body screamed at her to invite him straight back.

When he'd finally settled himself, Keren knew perfectly well that, this time, he'd positioned himself so he lay right at the edge of his half.

God help her, she *ached* to inch her way back to him.

'Keren?'

'What?' she croaked.

'I'm right here if you want me.'

'Yannis?'

'Yes, *glyko mou*?'

'Shut up and go to sleep.'

His low chuckle seeped through her fevered skin and she squeezed her eyes tightly shut.

It took a good few minutes of silence before her lungs could take in anything like vaguely normal breaths and the danger of self-asphyxiation passed. But her heartbeats didn't settle. Her racing pulses didn't settle. The heat inside her continued to blaze painfully. The throbbing ache between her legs grew.

This was torture.

Slowly, Yannis's breathing deepened.

He'd fallen asleep.

She could scream.

Yannis had always been able to fall asleep at will but for him to fall asleep now while she lay there ablaze with desire was cruelty personified.

She didn't know what she wanted to do most. Roll over and kick him for putting her in this frustrated state. Or roll over and crush herself against him and seek the relief of his mouth and…

She squeezed her eyes even tighter to drive the image out but it was no use.

If Yannis were to so much as press the tip of his finger to her, she would melt for him. She'd already melted. Lava flowed through her veins, not blood.

Without thinking, she rolled onto her back.

She turned her face to him. The thin stream of moonlight through the darkness allowed her to see his strong, masculinely beautiful features. Moisture replaced the dryness of her mouth and throat.

Her hand inched its way to his sleeping face. She snatched it back before her finger could press against his lips.

She *couldn't* make the first move. It would give him everything he wanted. Yannis had engineered everything for this moment and she couldn't just give in and put herself on a plate for him. Not after everything. What little pride she had left would be smashed to smithereens.

Before her body could take back control of her brain, Keren pushed the duvet off and climbed out of bed. Fixing her gaze on the bedroom door, she padded quietly to it then slipped out, too scared that she'd find his eyes open to look back. She took not a single breath until she'd softly closed the door behind her.

Then she climbed the stairs to the second

floor and raced to the other side of the villa, as far from him as she could get.

She hurried to the high window of the guest room she'd chosen as her sanctuary, and flung it open, then settled on the wide windowsill praying for her fevered skin to cool.

Had her escape woken him? Was he, at this very moment, seeking her out?

The thought had barely formed in her brain when the handle turned and the door opened and Yannis's silhouette appeared in the doorway.

Keren jumped off the ledge.

He stepped towards her.

She tried to step back. The ledge stopped her.

He didn't say a word until he was stood before her, eyes piercing wickedly straight through her. 'Hiding from me, *glyko mou*?'

Her legs were trembling. Her heart was swollen and pounding hard. She couldn't breathe. She couldn't speak.

And then she saw that, for all the nonchalance of his husky words, Yannis, too, was struggling for breath and her heart broke free from its confines and soared.

Understanding flowed between them.

His throat moved a number of times before

he speared his hand into her hair and cupped the back of her head. He gazed into her eyes for a long, breathless moment and then his lips vanquished hers with an intensity that scorched her into a burst of flames.

CHAPTER NINE

KEREN HAD FLED to this room knowing deep down that Yannis would follow her. Knowing he would recognise her hiding in the room as Keren making the first move. Knowing he would make the next one.

The firmness of his smooth lips moved against hers and then she felt the flicker of his velvet tongue against hers and the last of her consciousness vanished.

Crushing herself against his steel-hard frame, she rose onto her toes and wound her arms around his neck, fisting his hair as their kiss deepened into a fierce, hungry duel. The lava in her veins surged through her, deafening her ears, melting her core. Greedy fingers dragged over her back and down to her bottom clasping a buttock to pull her even closer.

Scratching his neck, she gasped into his mouth as she felt the hard ridge of his erection press into her stomach. Knowing that it wouldn't be long until that part of him was inside her turned her gasp into a moan.

Oh, but she wanted this so badly. Needed it. Yannis. His touch. Him. And how badly she wanted rid of her nightdress to feel his flesh against hers without any barrier.

He must have sensed her need for a breeze whipped around her calves and then her thighs as he bunched her nightdress up to her buttocks, the fusion of his mouth finally breaking when he stepped back just enough to raise her arms and whip the offending item off her and drop it without pause.

His breathing was heavy and ragged as he dipped his gaze over her, now as naked as he.

'*Theos*, Keren,' he groaned, cupping her face in his hands. 'You are so beautiful.' And then his mouth claimed her again, almost furious in its intensity, and their arms wrapped around each other tightly, naked flesh finally meeting naked flesh, her sensitised breasts finally getting their wish, flattened against his burning skin.

Giant hands gripped her hips. Her belly dipped then her feet left the ground. A moment later and they were on the bed, Yannis on top of her, his mouth continuing its heady assault. The need in her pelvis was so tightly coiled that she automatically wrapped her legs around his waist and raised her buttocks, but his mouth wrenched from her lips to trail down her neck. His hands swept down her waist to her hips and then back up over her stomach and ribs to cup her breasts at the same moment he flicked his tongue over a puckered nipple. When he took the peak into his hot mouth and sucked with a savagery that made her hips jerk, the cry that flew from her mouth echoed around the walls.

Writhing frantically beneath him, her fingers pulled at his hair and she arched her back, desperate for his possession, but the assault of his mouth continued, lips scorching their trail down her stomach until his face was buried between her legs and his tongue snaked between her folds to settle on the nub of her pleasure.

Her head flopped back and she closed her eyes, submitting entirely to the rapture of his mouth and tongue, the coil of need winding tighter and tighter, her fingers no longer pulling at his hair but buried in it, urging him on. For the first time in so, so long, the swell of an orgasm was rising inside her but, just as she reached the pinnacle, Yannis broke away.

In moments he was on top of her, his face hovering over hers. Immediately she wound her legs around his waist and arched into the tip of his erection, but he held back, snatching at her hands and pressing them either side of her head.

The tendons on his neck were strained, his jaw taut as his liquid gaze burned into her.

'Tell me you want this,' he demanded hoarsely.

'Yannis...*please*...' she wailed.

'*Tell* me.'

In answer, she raised her head and nipped his bottom lip with her teeth. 'You know I want this.'

The words had hardly left her mouth before he thrust. Keren was so wet and ready for him that in one long, exhilarating motion he was deep inside her.

Yannis groaned, then stilled. Deep blue eyes still locked on hers momentarily lost their focus before he blinked sharply and kissed her. Tongues entwined in a hot, ferocious duel, he began to move. In and out he thrust, deeper and deeper, harder and harder, each stroke and each grind tightening the coiled tension in her core.

Sensing that he was fighting back release, Keren urged him on, nails scraping over his back, mouth fusing to his cheek, his taut neck, his shoulder. The slickness of their skin melded together as the pinnacle grew closer and closer until the coil deep inside her unwound in a bullet of spiralling ecstasy that had her clinging to him, crying out his name and begging him to never let her go, never let her go, never let her go...

Yannis grabbed hold of her hips, threw his head back and, with a low, guttural sound reverberating out of his throat, gave one last violent thrust and then his sweat-slicked body collapsed on her.

The thuds of Keren's heart reverberated loudly in her ears. The thuds of Yannis's heart thumped through their crushed chests. The heat of his ragged breath burned into her neck.

The blissful thrills of their coupling were lessening inside her but a cauldron of emotions was bubbling in their place. Hot tears stabbed the back of her eyes, and she squeezed them tightly shut to stop them spilling out. In her head she repeated the mantra, *Don't cry, don't cry, don't cry.*

The last time they'd made love was over two years ago. Keren had been heavily pregnant. The further into the pregnancy she'd gone, the slower and gentler their lovemaking had become, a far cry from the heady rampancy that had consumed them in their early days but every bit as fulfilling. That last time had been tender and loving. She'd fallen asleep with Yannis's hand pressed to her swollen belly.

His possessiveness had first properly made itself known in the pregnancy but she had liked it, she remembered. Yannis had looked out for her with a solicitude that had made her feel cherished as well as loved.

A deep wrench tore through her heart and she clenched her jaw as tightly as she could to counter it, her fingers reflexively tightening their grip on his hair, which she had been absently running through.

How had they got it all so horribly wrong?

Would things be different if she went back to him? Could they return to how they'd been before…?

Frightened at the turn of her thoughts, Keren gave herself a mental slap. One orgasm and it wasn't just her body that had melted for him but her brain too. It had softened her completely. She needed to harden herself back up and quickly.

But when Yannis shifted his weight from her, she only just stopped herself rolling with his movement and cuddling up with her head on his chest and draping her legs over him like she always used to do after making love.

Swallowing hard, she turned her back to him. He spooned into her and hugged an arm around her, pulling her to him. She couldn't stop herself from taking his hand and holding it close.

The beats of her heart ramped up again.

Usually after making love, Yannis liked to talk. Light, playful nonsense mostly, making her grin as she fell into sleep. So far, he hadn't uttered a word and the longer his silence went on, the more unnerved she grew.

'This doesn't mean I'm coming back to you,' she said as evenly as she could manage.

He hugged her even closer and kissed the top of her head. 'Let's not talk about that any more. You are here and I am here—let's just enjoy it without any pressure, okay?'

Scared her swelling heart was going to choke her, she brought his hand to her mouth and kissed it.

Closing her eyes, she listened as Yannis's breaths made their familiar deepening into sleep. A long time later, she finally drifted off too, her last conscious thought that this was the most right she'd felt in two years.

A mouth brushed gently to hers pulled Keren from the fog of sleep. Her lips parted in welcome.

Caught in a dreamlike state, she didn't open her eyes until she lay replete, Yannis still inside her breathing heavily against her ear.

Smiling, she closed her eyes and drifted away again.

When Keren next opened her eyes, Yannis's side of the bed was empty. She looked at her watch then sat bolt upright. Ten a.m.! She hadn't slept so late in what felt like for ever.

Stretching first, she retrieved the Victorian nightgown from the floor, pulled it over her head and padded back to their bedroom. Her limbs felt all liquid. Her skin buzzed. Tiny throbs of deliciousness pulsed between her legs.

After a long shower, she had a quick root through her wardrobe and selected a floaty, sunshine orange summer dress with thin straps and which fell above her knees. She couldn't for the life of her think why she hadn't taken this dress with her when she left.

And then she remembered that Yannis had bought it for her on their honeymoon. He'd awoken early and, not wanting to wake her, left her sleeping while he went to explore the surrounding area. He'd spotted the dress and known immediately that she would love it. He'd been right.

Pressing a hand to her suddenly ragged heart, she took a long, deep breath then, face unadorned and her hair damp around her shoulders, left their room.

The languidness of her mood gone, she paused at Sophia's door and pressed her hand to her heart again.

How did Yannis cope walking past this empty room every day?

Keren hadn't coped. She saw that now. Some days, she would reach the nursery door and find her legs incapable of moving another inch and her lungs too tight to take in air. Palpitations and the agony of the banshee's screams locked in her head had come close to crippling her.

She covered the door handle, closed her eyes, counted to three then opened it. She made another count to three before she forced her eyes open.

For a moment she was too dazed to do anything but blink frantically.

She'd been so certain she would find the nursery stripped bare and repainted but it was all there, exactly as it had been when she'd last stepped foot in it. A beautiful haven waiting to be brought to life with a baby's gurgle.

But the baby had gone to heaven instead.

Brushing a tear away, she fought the swell

of emotions fighting to break free and walked back into the corridor, softly closing the door behind her.

Keren found Yannis where she'd guessed he would be—working off his chocolate mousse consumption via laps of the swimming pool.

Taking a seat on the poolside terrace, she helped herself to a coffee from the *briki* and leaned back, watching his powerful body strike through the water like lightning.

A long sigh escaped her lips.

How familiar and yet how alien this all was. But how right.

That's what she'd always felt with Yannis. A completeness. That he was hers and she was his. Her heart thrummed to imagine it could be like that for them again.

Could it really? Could they fall in love again, but this time do it right?

Was she already in love with him? Had her love for him ever really died?

She didn't know the answers. She was too scared to probe her feelings too deeply. What if it was just sex making her feel like this?

And what of Yannis's feelings for her? Was it just his pride that wanted her back or something more fundamental?

If it was just his pride then she would get back on her boat Monday morning and sail away.

She couldn't put her heart back on a plate for him only to watch him slip away from her again. She would not watch his love for her fade away and his hate spring back to life. She would not let the hate that had formed for him in her broken heart contaminate her again.

To go through that again would break her into pieces with no hope of repair.

But if there was a chance for them…

She watched as he heaved himself out of the pool without bothering to use the steps. Her heart turned from a thrum into a thud.

Snatching his towel off the tiled pool surround, he strode to her, a wide grin on his gorgeous face, drying himself as he went.

He leaned over and kissed her mouth, then, eyes gleaming, poured himself a coffee and took the seat next to her.

'You, *glyko mou*, look good enough to eat.'

'Maybe later.'

The devil appeared in his blue eyes before he kissed her again, harder, fingers gripping her waist. 'No *maybe*.' Then he nipped the lobe of her ear and leaned back in his seat, his gaze telling her clearly the lasciviousness of his thoughts.

Keren crossed her legs and pressed her thighs tightly together in a futile effort to dampen her flourishing desire.

'Hungry?' he asked, raising a sinful brow.

'Starving,' she replied, and not just as a double entendre. She couldn't remember the last time she'd had such an appetite and she wasn't so delusional that she didn't know where it had come from. Yannis's lovemaking. It had melted her bones, turned her brain to mush and awoken long-suppressed appetites.

His lips quirked seductively. 'I thought so. Breakfast should be served... Now.'

As if by magic, the same young man who'd served their dinner appeared with their breakfast and a fresh *briki* of coffee.

'What would you like to do today?' Yannis asked after she'd eaten every scrap of her omelette and was busy devouring a bowl of yogurt and honey. 'Go back to bed and stay there?'

She sighed and resisted the urge to lean into him and kiss him. As right as this all felt and as deeply as her veins burned for his touch, she had to keep her feet grounded. It would be too easy to succumb and allow her heart to spring free.

His phone rang from the other side of the table.

He rolled his eyes and stretched an arm to reach it. Then he frowned. 'It's Andreas. I'd better answer it.'

Leaning back into his seat, he dived straight into conversation with his brother. From the darkening of his eyes and tone, Keren guessed it was more bad news.

'What's happened?' she asked when he'd ended the call.

He rubbed his jaw. 'A potential client we were at the contract stage with has decided to go with Hoults instead of us.'

Her heart sank for him. Two clients in two days was, as far as she knew, unprecedented. 'I'm sorry.'

He nodded grimly and raised his head back to breathe deeply.

'Did they say why?'

'I missed an appointment with them.'

Her eyes widened. That was not like Yannis. He despised tardiness, was punctual to a fault.

'When was the appointment?'

He shook his head. 'It doesn't matter,' he muttered. Then he took another deep breath and fixed his attention back to her. As their eyes locked together, the sensual gleam returned. Twisting in his chair so their knees touched, he gripped her thighs. His strength and speed were such that she only realised he'd pulled her onto his lap when she was actually on it, straddling him. Through the lace of her knickers, she felt his excitement grow at warp speed and her breaths quickened at the same rate.

'I need to be inside you. Let's go back to bed,' he urged.

Heat already bubbling, she wrapped her arms around his neck and razed her teeth into his cheek.

Holding her securely, he stood, lifting her with him. He carried her like that all the way to their bedroom.

Keren laid her head back against the bath's roll-top. A swell of contentment rolled through her.

Contentment was an emotion she hadn't felt in a long, long time.

'What are you thinking?' Yannis asked casually.

They'd adopted the position they'd long ago discovered worked best for them when sharing a bath: facing each other, Yannis's legs bent, his calves resting against her waist, Keren's much smaller legs stretched out against his sides, her feet resting on his chest.

Keeping her eyes closed, she serenely answered, 'That silence is golden.'

'Not thinking about how much you want to come over here?'

'I'm good, thanks.'

'Not even for this?'

She opened one eye.

His shameless erection poked through the bubbles.

Eyes smouldering, he said, 'Want to play?'

'Didn't your mother ever tell you that if you play with something too much, it eventually breaks?'

His grin was wicked. 'Since when do I listen to my mother?'

'Speaking of your mother…'

'Do we have to?'

'Is that Legarde woman still going to the fund-raiser tonight?'

'As far as I know. Why?'

'I think you should go.'

His eyebrow rose in bemusement. 'Are you joking with me?'

'You need to be there.'

'Andreas can handle it,' he dismissed, but not before she caught the flicker in his eye.

'Not as well as you can. Your mind is more forensic than his.'

'I'm not leaving you,' he stated flatly.

'Then take me with you.'

'Now I *know* you are joking.'

'I'm not.'

'You would come?'

She shrugged. 'It's important. If you weren't holding me captive, you'd already be in Athens.'

The gleam came back in his eyes and the torpedo rose back up. 'Holding you captive, am I?'

'Bar the handcuffs.'

'Our old pair are still around somewhere. I can—'

She poked his chest with her toe. 'Stop changing the subject. Are we going or what?'

'I'd much rather cuff you to the bed. *That* will stop you leaving on Monday.'

'Maybe by Monday I won't want to leave.'

His features tightened in an instant. All amusement and sensuality evaporated from his eyes, replaced with an intensity that burned through her.

Impulse had Keren spring forward. Water sloshed everywhere as she clambered on top of him and cupped his cheeks.

Not for the first time she imagined herself drowning in the blue of his eyes.

'Yannis, I don't know how I feel, okay?' she said softly. 'This time yesterday I wanted nothing to do with you, but you touch me and I turn to goo, and now my head is all over the place. I don't know if it's sex making me feel differently about you, so I'm not going to make any promises. We can't go back to the way things were. I can't be trapped in a cage.'

And she didn't know if she could forgive him for finding emotional solace with someone else or forget his maliciousness after she left.

'I know,' he whispered, knotting a fist into her hair. 'Losing Sophia—'

Keren quickly put a finger to his lips and shook her head. *No. Not now. Not like this.*

His jaw clenched. His gaze held hers as if searching for something, but then his features softened and his lips curved into a rueful smile, and he nodded his understanding.

She hadn't realised her shoulders had tightened until they loosened, and she pressed her lips to his.

No one understood her like Yannis did.

She deepened the fusion of their mouths. How she loved the dark taste of his kisses. The way he kissed her told her how much he loved the taste of her kisses too. Their first kiss had been her first real kiss. She'd thought she would combust from the sensory explosion of that first kiss, had had no idea of all the other, even headier sensations he would elicit in her, that she would become a walking, talking tinderbox of lust.

Palming her cheeks, Yannis gently pushed her face away and stared into her eyes. 'I will never try to cage you again, I swear.'

She sighed. She yearned to believe him but promises made in the steam of lust evaporated quickly. They'd had this before and they'd lost it all.

And yet, gazing into eyes brimming with emotion that contained more than mere desire, her heart softened then expanded and another emotion she hadn't felt in so, so long slipped in.

Hope.

Maybe she was losing her mind in this steam of lust. She no longer cared. The one thing—the only thing—she was certain about was this thick, consuming desire that had drugged them both, and she threaded her fingers through his hair, closed her eyes and moulded her lips back to his, crushing herself as tightly to him as she could.

The passion of his response only stoked

the furnace burning in her core. His mouth plundered hers as if her kisses were the air he needed to breathe, his hands roaming everywhere, sweeping her back, her sides, grasping her bottom, leaving a trail of sensation in their wake.

Breathing heavily, Keren pulled away from his mouth and danced her fingers down his throat to rest on his chest, moving her thighs to straddle him. She raised herself a little higher. His erection jutted against her folds.

She'd always adored making love by daylight because it meant she could soak in and revel in Yannis. And she'd loved to see the evidence of his desire for her etched on his face.

It was etched there now.

One hand now holding her waist tightly, he trailed a finger all the way down from the base of her throat to the top of her pubis, then he slipped it lower still, liquid eyes becoming hooded when he found her swollen and ready for him. But he gave her no relief, snaking the finger back up over her belly to lightly skim the underside of her breast before taking its weight in his hand. When he flickered a thumb over a puckered nipple, she cried out at the painful pleasure of it, and sank desperately onto his length.

Eyes wide on his, Keren held his shoulders tightly, raised herself up then sank back down. Sensations infused every last inch of her. The coil in her core tensed to a point.

Yannis cupped her whole breast and squeezed with just the right amount of pressure to make her cry out again.

'That's it, you beautiful creature.' His voice was ragged. Husky. 'Let go.'

The moan that came from her mouth sounded wild amongst the roaring of blood in her ears as she lost all control of herself, riding him with wanton abandon, nails digging into his flesh, his groans of pleasure feeding her until ecstasy burst through and all she could see was Yannis's face flickering in the white light.

CHAPTER TEN

'I'D FORGOTTEN HOW good you look in a tux,' Keren said, feasting her eyes over Yannis as she stepped from her dressing room into the bedroom. Sexy whatever he did— or didn't—wear, there was something about him dressed formally that always made her insides clench with pleasure. That late afternoon, he'd donned a navy tuxedo and black bow tie and it fitted his tall, rock-hard frame like a glove. Which was just as well as it had been handstitched. Freshly shaven, hair quiffed, he looked swarthy enough to be the star in his own spy thriller.

'Me?' Yannis shook his head, eyes roaming over her. '*Theos*, you look stunning, *glyko mou.*'

Feeling suddenly anxious, she only just stopped herself from biting into her bottom lip and ruining her freshly applied red lipstick. 'You're sure?'

And now she remembered that this is how it had always been before. She would select an item of clothing to wear to a function like this, get dressed and then ask Yannis's opinion. And then get hurt when he gave an honest answer, especially in those last few months when she'd deliberately chosen more and more provocatively inappropriate outfits.

It had been deliberate, she realised painfully. Deliberate but not conscious. She'd been trying to provoke him into showing her emotion. Any emotion. She'd been desperate for him to show he still felt something, *anything*, for her as a woman.

The dress she'd chosen was far removed from the haute couture the other ladies were bound to be wearing that night, but it was a dress she loved. With off-the-shoulder sleeves that tied in puffed bows just below the elbow, it was white with blood-red roses patterned on it. Floating to mid-calf in bohemian fashion, the skirt had a split in one side that ran to mid-thigh. She'd paired it with four-inch blood-red sandals whose straps criss-crossed over her feet.

Having not worn anything but flip-flops and flat sandals in eighteen months, she'd spent ten minutes practising walking in them in her dressing room while at the same time trying to remember how she'd used to sweep her hair back into an informal but reasonably elegant chignon.

Once she was ready, she'd held her wedding and engagement rings in the palm of her hand. She'd come so close to sliding them on her finger. She'd wanted to. Desperately. But she wasn't ready. Not yet. Instead, she'd placed them on the dressing table and then opened her jewellery box and finally allowed the memories contained within it to soak into her. She'd selected the pair of chunky gold hooped earrings Yannis had bought her to celebrate their first month together and three solid gold bracelets that glittered under the light.

His chest rose sharply and his throat moved. His nostrils flared before he said, simply, 'You're beautiful. You're always beautiful. And that dress is beautiful too.'

The anxiety breathed away from her and she smiled. 'And that, my love, is the correct answer.'

He didn't return the smile. 'I should never have criticised you. I think…' He sighed and ran his fingers through his hair. 'I went too far. I wanted to protect you from the cattiness of my world. I forgot you didn't need my protection. Not in that respect.' His shoulders rose and he grimaced. 'I fell in love with *you* and I will regret making you feel that you weren't good enough exactly as you are for the rest of my life. Because you were. Good enough. You were perfect exactly as you were. You still are.'

Her heart almost breaking and choking in one confused wrench, Keren walked carefully to him in her four-inch heels and placed a hand on a shoulder she knew was marked afresh from her nails.

'You've messed your hair up,' she said softly. 'Lean forward.'

He bowed his head.

Working with the tips of her fingers, she carefully put it back into place, letting the scent of his freshly applied cologne infuse her senses. No one in the world smelled as good as Yannis.

'There,' she said when she was done.

He took a hand and brought it to his lips. 'Thank you.' Then he smiled, the old devilish look returning to his eyes. 'We should leave now before I give in to temptation and rip that dress from you to devour what's underneath. But the car is waiting for us.'

Threading her fingers through his, she rubbed her nose to his neck. 'You'll just have to wait until we get back.'

'If I can…'

'You can,' she assured him.

Hands clasped together, they left their room.

Keren's stomach made its usual plunge when they passed the nursery. Some unbidden impulse had her blurt out the question that had woven in and out of her mind throughout the day. 'Why did you keep it all?'

She didn't have to explain any further.

'I didn't have the right. It was a decision for both of us when the time was right,' he explained simply. 'What do you think we should do with it? We can—'

'We can talk about it another time,' she interrupted hastily. 'Let's just concentrate on you dealing with cow-face Legarde and me dealing with your parents.'

She felt his scrutiny but kept her gaze fixed on the approaching staircase.

'You are nervous about seeing them?'

'A bit. Your mother's nails are very long and sharp.'

'Her tongue's sharper.'

'Thanks for the reminder. Do they hate me?'

'No.'

They'd reached the bottom of the staircase. She stopped walking and looked at his face to see if he was telling the truth.

'*No,*' he repeated with more force. 'They don't hate you. They will be glad to see you.'

'Have you told them I'm coming?'

'I told Andreas. He's passed the message on… And I forgot to tell you he'll be meeting us at the airfield.'

'Good.' Keren had always got on brilliantly with Yannis's older brother and especially brilliantly with his husband. Then a thought smacked into her. 'My passport!'

Private jet or not, Agon was a sovereign country and entering mainland Greece required a passport. Her passport was in her grab-bag on her boat.

Yannis's responding wide grin immediately filled her with suspicion.

'What?'

He reached into the inside pocket of his dinner jacket and removed two passports.

Keren plucked them from his hand. The first one she flipped open had her unsmiling face in it.

'You've had this all the time?' she asked, confused.

He shrugged. 'It wasn't safe to keep it on the boat.'

'But how did you know where to find it?'

'You're a woman who thinks of safety first.

It made sense you would keep it where you could easily get hold of if needed.'

'It was in a waterproof bag.'

'The bag is in my safe.'

Putting her hands on her hips, she stared at him with disbelief. 'So you've had my passport, phone and money here all this time? And you let me believe it was still on the boat?'

He didn't look the slightest bit abashed. 'I did offer for you to put the divorce papers in the safe. If you'd trusted me with them, you would have seen your bag was in there.'

She shook her head. 'You're unbelievable.'

'I think the word you mean is *incredible*. And yes, I am.'

'No, I definitely mean unbelievable.'

'All is fair in love and war, *glyko mou*.'

'You think?'

'I *know*.'

'I'll make sure to remember that.'

But, no matter how indignantly prim she held her chin aloft as she followed him out to the waiting car, Keren couldn't deny the thrills of joy racing through her veins.

All's fair in love and war.

Love…

Yannis's parents' home in Athens was an imposing neoclassical building set in the old quarter of Plaka, known locally as the neighbourhood of the gods, close to the Acropolis museum. Keren had loved the bustling area that effortlessly combined ancient archaeology and vibrant culture so much that they'd spoken about buying a home there for themselves.

She'd also loved Nina and Aristidis's sprawling terracotta courtyard garden. Filled with delights that included ancient statues and potted olive trees older than her grandparents, it was like stepping into ancient Greece, but with a modern twist, a garden far different to what she'd expected from a couple who thrived on stuffy formality.

The courtyard was already filled with people and noise when they arrived with Andreas and Pavlos, and the knotting of her stomach betrayed to Keren how nervous she was about this evening. She doubted there would be many people there she hadn't met before or who didn't know that she and Yannis were divorcing, and she braced herself for amazed looks and whispers behind hands.

She couldn't see through the crowd to find the two people she was most nervous about seeing. Yannis's parents. For all that he insisted they didn't hate her, she didn't imagine they would be as welcoming as his brother had been. Andreas had greeted her with a tight hug and a whispered, 'It is so good to see you.' Pavlos's embrace had practically choked the life out of her.

The knot in her belly tightened when she caught sight of the tall, swarthy man approaching them. The top of the head of his coiffured wife bobbed beside him.

And then they were standing before them.

They embraced their two sons and Pavlos, Andreas's husband, without even looking at her. But then they fixed their attention on her.

Every eye in the courtyard was watching them.

Keren held her breath and tried not to wilt under the weight of their scrutiny. There was something almost symbiotic about Nina and Aristidis's body language, something she thought must come from the long, enduring strength of their marriage. Her parents were the same.

She was still holding her breath when a smile, tentative to begin with, broke out on Nina's face and then Keren found herself pulled into a tight, perfumed embrace that squeezed the air she'd been holding out of her lungs.

'It is wonderful to have you home, *kope-*

lia mou,' Nina said. 'We have missed you very much.'

There was no time to take this in for Aristidis wanted in on the act and, with Nina keeping hold of Keren's hand, planted a dozen kisses to her face.

Utterly thrown at such heartfelt greetings, Keren responded in kind. If she thought this was an act for their audience, the tears shining in Nina's eyes told her otherwise and she found herself blinking back tears of her own.

Not in a million years had she expected that.

So much for them throwing parties to celebrate her departure.

As the crowd had drawn in around them, there were too many other people wanting to embrace her for Keren to properly think about this startling turn of events but by the time things had settled and she'd been handed a Santorini Sunrise cocktail, the knot in her belly had loosened and she could breathe properly.

As the function was a fund-raiser for Nina and Aristidis's latest pet project, socialising was soon put to one side. Tonight, they were hosting an auction, one that was very different from the auctions the Filipidises specialised in. Rows of chairs had been set out in a horseshoe at the far end of the courtyard and everyone was invited to take their seats.

Aristidis took the auctioneer mantle and soon the most ridiculous array of lots were being furiously fought over for the most ridiculous sums. When Yannis got in a bidding war for a set of children's Japanese cartoon trading cards, Keren found herself laughing harder than she'd laughed in the longest time.

She'd forgotten that even high society could poke fun at itself.

She'd forgotten a lot of things. Like Nina's tenderness when they'd lost Sophia.

When Keren had eventually been discharged from hospital, she'd returned home to find Nina had moved in. For two weeks, her mother-in-law had cared for her with the same kind of love her own mother would have given her. Later, Keren had learned that the only reason her mother hadn't flown out to be with her—and that would have been a huge thing for her as both her parents had found flying to Agon for their wedding the most terrifying experience of their lives—had been because Nina had promised she would look after Keren for her.

How could she have forgotten that?

And how could she have forgotten the words Aristidis had whispered after the funeral? *'Don't fight the grief,* kopelia mou. *If it gets too much, Nina and I are always here for you. You're our daughter and we love you.'*

She blinked frantically, suddenly terrified, both from the tears that were burning to be set free and from the tempest of emotions the memories were evoking.

The next lot was for a pair of tatty plastic sunflowers and Keren fought hard to keep up with the spirit of the auction and applaud when a financier paid twenty thousand euros for them.

'Are you okay?' Yannis asked, leaning in to whisper in her ear.

She pasted a smile to her face and nodded with as much enthusiasm as she could feign.

'Sure?'

She squeezed his hand then released it to clap enthusiastically along with everyone else over the sale of something she'd missed.

'Which one's Jeanie Legarde?' she asked, groping desperately for conversation to distract her.

'Don't make it obvious that you're looking, but two rows behind us to your left—the silver-haired woman wearing horn-rimmed glasses.'

She waited until her curiosity got too much and turned her head as discreetly as she could. She clocked who he meant immediately, and as her eyes landed on the woman's face, she was taken by the strong urge to leap over the seated people between them and slap her.

The violence of her reaction to a woman she hadn't even spoken to frightened her.

'Stop staring,' Yannis chided quietly, taking her hand again.

Breathing deeply, Keren tore her stare away and dragged her attention to the final lot of the auction.

What had caused that reaction? The fact that Jeanie Legarde was threatening to use a rival auction house? That was business. It wasn't personal. Yannis and Andreas would talk to her that evening and they would change her mind with the effortless charm, expertise and nous that had served the Filipidises so well for centuries.

Blood whooshed in her head, dizzying her as she realised why she felt so hateful towards the French lady. It was because she was messing Yannis around and, for Keren, that had always felt personal even when it had been business. He used to tell her tales of difficult clients and she'd secretly longed to get revenge on them for him. Once, he'd brought a particularly obnoxious client who'd driven him to distraction to their home for dinner and she'd had to resist spitting in his food.

That had been when they'd been a team, because once, they *had* been a team. It hadn't been perfect but it had been heavenly all the same, their imperfections nothing more than the rough that needed to be taken with the smooth.

Then the smooth had disappeared and Yannis had turned away from her and the love they'd shared had turned into hate...

Except that a tiny grain of her love for him had lodged itself tight in that hate, and that tiny grain had burst out at the sight of him. Being back with him, making love, just *being* with him, had overloaded her senses with Yannis's essence, giving the grain the nourishment it needed to bloom back into spring.

Didn't that grain deserve the chance to see summer again? Didn't *they* deserve that chance? Wasn't the truth that though she'd been as free as a macaw without him, she'd never once felt a jot of the happiness she'd experienced with him when things had been good?

But wasn't the truth, too, that her misery in those last months with him had been the hardest she'd ever had to endure? Could she really risk opening herself to that again?

She watched him rise from his seat with her heart pounding and a sick feeling in her stomach that she wasn't sure was a good sick or a bad sick.

Could she do it? Give her heart back to him? Trust that he wouldn't neglect it and then turn his back on it? Trust that he wouldn't try and suffocate her again?

Trust that he wanted her back for *her*?

'We're going to have a chat with a certain Ms Legarde,' Yannis murmured.

Keren blinked herself back to the present and saw Andreas and Pavlos had joined them. She swallowed. 'Good luck.'

He winked. 'No luck needed.' Then he swiped a kiss over her mouth and strode off, his brother at his side.

'Drink?' Pavlos asked.

Expelling a breath, she nodded, glad that he was with her. Pavlos was one of her favourite people in the world. They'd always tried to rig the seating at functions they'd both attended, be it business or personal, to ensure they were seated next to each other.

Swiping the pair of them a Santorini Sunrise from a passing waitress, Pavlos lead her to a circular table which was a little more secluded than the others and which gave them a good view of Yannis and Andreas chatting to Jeanie Legarde. Nothing in their body language hinted at tension.

No sooner had they sat than Nina and her sister, Ariadne, joined them. Keren had missed Ariadne earlier and was overcome with gratitude to be swept up in another bear hug.

Nina sat beside her and inched her chair as close as she could get, holding Keren's hand tightly as if afraid to let her go.

'It really is good to have you here again,' she said in a low voice once Ariadne and Pavlos were deep in conversation. 'I have prayed every day for you to come home.'

Her throat closing, Keren could only stare into the blue eyes Nina's youngest son had inherited.

Nina covered the hand she was holding and squeezed. 'Today is the first time I've seen Yannis smile since you left.'

'Nina!'

They all turned their heads to see Aristidis, holding court with a group of self-important men, beckoning his wife.

Nina gave Keren the faintest of winks, kissed her cheek and left to join her husband.

Keren moved her chair closer to Pavlos and joined in the conversation until Ariadne went off to mingle, leaving them alone with a pair of fresh cocktails.

'How do you think it's going?' Keren asked, nodding at Yannis and Andreas, who were still in deep conversation with Jeanie Legarde.

His eyes narrowed slightly in contemplation. 'They all seem relaxed.'

As he said this, Jeanie suddenly threw her head back and laughed.

Keren met Pavlos's eye and they both laughed.

The easy conversation they'd always found together resumed as if they'd never parted and soon Pavlos was filling her in on all the gossip she'd missed. Keren had never cared for gossip but Pavlos was so funny in the way he told his stories that, for him, she was happy to make an exception.

While he regaled her, she kept looking over at Yannis at the other side of the courtyard. The conversation between the three of them showed no sign of letting up and yet every time she looked over, it was as if he sensed her gaze on him for his eyes would flicker over to her. Even with the distance between them, the flicker of his gaze heated her veins with a frisson of arousal and she found herself having to really concentrate on Pavlos's chatter and not succumb to fantasies about what would happen when she and Yannis got back to the villa…

'How did you find living on water?'

Pavlos's swerve from gossip to personal was entirely expected. She was only surprised it had taken him so long.

She had a drink of her cocktail. 'I love it.'

He nudged her with his elbow. 'That's a *terrible* answer.'

She laughed. 'Be more specific, then!'

'Where did you sail to? What were your favourite places?'

'I mostly sailed the Caribbean then I moved on to Europe before the hurricane season started. I was thinking of doing the South Pacific next.'

'*Was* thinking? You're planning to stay? For good?'

She bit into her lip. The truth was, she was torn. How could she trust herself to make the right decision? She'd followed her heart with Yannis before and all it had brought her was pain. But the thought of leaving him again…

That *hurt*.

Whatever she decided to do, she couldn't have this conversation with Pavlos before she had it with Yannis.

Even in his inebriated state—Pavlos was now on his fourth cocktail since they'd sat at the table—he must have read something in her expression for he smiled widely. 'Thank God for that!'

'Pav, please, I can't talk about this.'

He rolled his eyes huffily. 'Okay, but before we change the subject, and as I have you to myself, can I just say that if you *are* staying...' He winked. 'Then I thank the Lord, because your husband has been a nightmare.'

Curiosity got the better of her. 'Has he? In what way?'

He pretended to shudder. 'Like Nina when she was going through the worst of the menopause.'

Biting her cheek to stop the burst of laughter that wanted to spring free, she gave him her best unamused look.

'Did I say something sexist?' he asked innocently.

'Lots of women would say so, but you were saying about Yannis being a nightmare,' she prompted.

'Just ugly behaviour,' he evaded.

'What kind of ugly behaviour?'

'You know the kind.' Then his eyes gleamed and he leaned in closer. 'Also, you coming back takes the pressure off us.'

'What pressure?'

'Aristidis and Nina are desperate for the

patter of little Filipidis feet. Aristidis keeps going on about the future and the need for an heir to carry on the business and the Filipidis name. Nina keeps dropping hints about adoption even though she knows we don't want children. I'm surprised she didn't greet you with a crown of orchids to promote your fertility and—' He cut himself off mid-flow and, clearly horrified, covered his mouth. 'Oh, Keren, I am so sorry. I got carried away. I…' He grabbed her hands and pulled them to him. 'Please, forgive me, it's just so great you being back here, and I've missed you so much, and I got carried away, and for a moment I forgot.'

'It's okay,' she assured him with no idea how she was able to keep her voice even. Pavlos hadn't meant any harm and she could tell how close he was to being drunk. His words were beginning to slur. A drunk Pavlos was an indiscreet Pavlos.

'It isn't. I should never have loaded that all on you, not after everything—'

'I said it's okay,' she interrupted sharply before he could build up another head of steam.

She couldn't bear to discuss Sophia in such a crowded place. She found it virtually impossible to talk about her as it was, but if she could, it should be with Yannis.

Yannis wanted to talk about her. She knew it. He'd tried but she'd steered him away. She just couldn't do it, could only stop the banshee screams that grew too loudly in her head at the mention of Sophia with questions that required monosyllabic answers.

'I'm sorry they've been pressurising you,' she said in a softer tone. It wasn't Pavlos's fault that talking about her lost daughter felt like having iced needles plunged into her heart. 'Has Yannis been getting it in the neck from them too?'

He grimaced and downed his cocktail. 'What do you think?'

Across the courtyard, she could see the conflab with Jeanie Legarde was over. The three of them were heading into the house. Yannis had brought the contract with him. She guessed Jeanie was going to sign it.

Pavlos indicated for another drink. 'They don't mean to put the pressure on—you know what they're like. It's what we signed up for when we agreed to marry their sons, isn't it? We agreed to become Filipidises. Andreas and I hadn't realised how much the pressure had been building on us until Yannis made his promise.'

'What promise?'

His fresh cocktail was delivered to him. He had a large drink of it and hiccupped.

She patted his back. 'Tell me about Yannis's promise,' she urged.

Taking another drink first, he explained, 'Aristidis called a family summit a few weeks ago. It turned into a big argument and ended with Andreas and Aristidis giving Yannis the ultimatum.'

Somehow, she managed to refrain from shaking his shoulders. 'Which was?'

'That he gets you back or gets kicked out of the business.'

CHAPTER ELEVEN

KEREN FORCED HERSELF to remain calm while she tried her best to take in everything Pavlos had just told her. Pavlos was drunk. She needed to be careful not to misinterpret him.

She leaned her face into his and, once his eyes were focused on her, quietly but precisely said, 'Have I got this right? Aristidis and Andreas told Yannis they were going to kick him out of the business if I didn't come back?'

He covered his mouth again.

She gritted her teeth. 'Yes or no?'

'Yes. But it's not like that. Not that bad. You know?'

'No, I don't know. I need you to tell me. You said Yannis's behaviour had been ugly. Is that the reason? Or is it the Filipidis heir thing? An ultimatum to produce the next generation?'

He shook his head. 'I can't. I'm sorry. I said too much. Andreas will kill me.'

'*I'll* kill you if you don't tell me!'

Expression pained, he finished his cocktail. 'It's not just the need for a Filipidis heir but—'

'Not *just*,' she pounced. Her heart pounced too, a painful pouncing kick against her ribs. 'But it did play a part in it. Yes or no?'

'Keren…'

Yannis, Andreas and Jeanie had emerged from the house and were now heading towards them.

How she stopped herself screaming in Pavlos's face she would never know. 'Yes or no?'

He closed his eyes.

'Yes or no?'

His eyes snapped open. '*Yes.*'

Three seconds later, Yannis and the others reached their table. Those three seconds were just long enough for Keren to slip a mask on her face and smile in greeting.

Yannis bowed his head, kissed her mouth then introduced her to Jeanie Legarde.

Seats were taken, more cocktails were brought to their table and soon they were joined by others, tables being pushed together, a happy summer evening filled with the filthy rich who'd collectively raised a huge sum of money for a very worthy cause and were now all intent on letting their hair down and enjoying the excellent Filipidis hospitality.

All except for Keren.

If her passport wasn't in Yannis's inside dinner jacket pocket, she would have slipped out of the house and made a run for it.

Nausea churned in her stomach making even the delicious-looking canapés revolt her. But she kept smiling. Kept up with conversation. Kept her expression animated. Pretended not to see the concern in Yannis's eyes every time she dared look at him. Pretended not to flinch at his touch.

Ants had been let loose on her skin and were crawling all over her. She wanted to crawl away and hide under a rock with them as escape and punishment at her stupidity.

She even managed to relate the tale, at Yannis's prompting, of how she came to be called Keren and not Karen. It was a tale he'd always found hilarious.

She left out the part about there being complications with her birth. She'd suffered from the same pregnancy high blood pressure issues her own mother had but the difference had been the outcome. Keren and her mother were both still here to tell the tale. But she had no wish to discuss that with anyone, let alone strangers.

'Mum had to stay in hospital for quite a while after having me,' she told them.

Ten days her mother spent there, two of them fighting for her life. Keren had gone through the same thing a generation later.

'So she sent my dad to register my birth. He dropped in at his workplace on the way there to share the good news and his workmates dragged him down the pub to celebrate—my dad's not a drinker so I'm pretty sure it's the only time he's ever said yes to that. By the time he got to the registry office he was drunk and slurring so much that the registrar misheard what he said my name was to be. When Dad realised the mistake, he was too embarrassed to correct it. It took him two months to confess to my mum,' she added with a grin to hide the unexpected wistfulness that clenched at her heart.

Her mum had been cross with her dad when he finally confessed but had grown to like it, had often told Keren what a pretty name it was and how well it suited her. Keren had always lived in hope her parents would accidentally try something else new and grow to like that too and now she felt another clench in her heart. For the first time in her life she wished she'd grown up to be a zebra finch like the rest of the Burridges.

If she had, she would have a nice stable job, probably in her home town, be dating a nice young man, probably also from her home town, be making plans to buy a home together or for their wedding, probably both. She would be comfortable and settled. The only danger of hurt would come from what her insurance policy called Acts of God.

She would get her boat back and then she would set sail for England, Keren decided. She hadn't seen her family since Christmas. They might not understand her in the slightest, but they had always *tried* to understand, and they had always supported her. They had always loved her.

The only person who had ever understood her was Yannis, but his support was a lie and she'd been a fool to hope that he might still love her.

He understood her so well he'd known exactly what to say and do to win her back. If not for a drunken Pavlos, she would have fallen for it.

It was late when they left Athens. Andreas and Pavlos changed their plans and shared their flight back on Yannis's jet, giving

Yannis and Andreas the opportunity to fill Keren—Pavlos zonked out before they were in the air—on what happened with Jeanie Legarde and how they'd coaxed her into changing her mind and auctioning her late brother's masterpieces with Filipidis Fine Art & Antiquities *and* without a drop in the commission. From the admiring looks Andreas kept shining on Yannis, the younger Filipidis brother had been the force behind the change of mind. From the relief in both brothers' faces compared to when they'd arrived, neither had had high hopes that they could change it.

Keren had never had any doubt that Yannis would talk Jeanie Legarde round. The man could talk a sea-wanderer into buying salt water. Once he fixed those striking blue eyes on someone and gave them his full attention, they were eating out of his hands in minutes. Even she, who'd built a fortress around her heart to protect herself from him, had seen the fortress bulldozed to ash in the space of a day.

Once they landed, Andreas and Pavlos jumped into Yannis's waiting car with them for a lift back to their apartment in Agon's main town. As Yannis's villa was closer to the airfield, his driver dropped him and

Keren back first. Even so, it was almost two o'clock in the morning when they finally arrived back.

Keren got out of the car and virtually sagged with the relief of being able to lose the bonhomie she'd maintained since Pavlos had dropped his bomb on her lap.

The relief was short-lived, a mere breath before she steeled herself for what must come next.

They hadn't even closed the villa door behind them when Yannis pulled her into his arms and crushed his mouth to hers.

Keren fisted her hands by her sides and fought the automatic sensory explosion that even the numbing of her mind was unable to prevent.

He pulled away and put his hands on her shoulders. 'What's wrong?'

She shrugged his hands off and summoned all her courage to look him in the eye.

She never wanted to gaze into those beautiful eyes again.

'I've decided I won't be staying. I'd be grateful if you could arrange for whoever stole my boat to return it to me. Now.'

Shock flared in his eyes and tics played out around his lips before they tugged into a smile. 'That is a good joke.'

'Not a joke,' she refuted evenly. Turning on her heel, she headed straight to Yannis's study. 'I'm leaving and I'm not coming back.'

The knots in her belly were coiled too tightly and her energy too drained from spending hours pretending everything was hunky-dory for her to cope with a confrontation or navel-gaze at her foolishness in falling for his cruel games. Yannis's maliciousness since she'd left him meant she should have known better.

He didn't hesitate to follow her. 'What's happened?'

'Why do you assume something's happened?'

'Because I'm not an idiot.'

'No,' she agreed. 'You're not. And neither am I.' She couldn't stop herself from bitterly adding, 'I know everything, Yannis.'

He snatched hold of her wrist before she could push open the study door. 'What do you think you know?'

Hating that her skin still burned joyously at his touch, Keren prised his fingers off and stared at him with all the contempt she could muster. 'That your father and brother gave you an ultimatum. Get me back so we can produce an heir or be kicked out of the business.'

His face turned ashen. His lips parted and his throat moved but no sound came out.

'Thank you for not denying it.' She gave a tight smile and stepped into the study.

'It was not like that,' he said hoarsely.

'Oh, so they didn't tell you to get me back?'

'Not like you think they said it.' He pulled at his hair. 'Let me fix you a drink. I will explain everything.'

Feeling that she really could be sick, she went to the safe. 'I don't want anything from you but my boat, now get your phone out and make that call and get my boat back to me.'

A tiny tear cut through her heart to find the code was the same as it had been when she'd lived there. Their wedding date.

She refused to let it halt her focus. Her grab-bag was in the safe, just as Yannis had said. Probably the only thing he hadn't lied about. She pulled it out and quickly checked the contents. Her phone and money were still in it. She dropped the red clutch bag she'd taken out with her that night and which she'd put her passport in on the return journey from Athens into it, and then checked her phone. Damn it, it had run out of charge.

She closed her eyes briefly and took a deep breath before turning back to face him.

He was standing like a statue, staring at

her. His features had tightened so much his cheekbones looked like they were about to poke through the skin.

'Make the call, Yannis.'

He cleared his throat. 'Keren…'

The pain from the tear that cut through her heart this time would have doubled her over if it hadn't released a bolt of the fury she'd been trying her best to contain. 'Make that call and give me back my boat!' she screamed. 'Make it now or I'm out of here and I don't care if it's the middle of the night. I'll walk to the police station barefoot if I have to and report it stolen, just give me back my boat!'

The pulse on his jaw was throbbing as strongly as she'd ever seen it, but she must have got through to him for, his eyes not leaving her face, he reached slowly into his inside jacket pocket and removed his phone. He held it up as if to prove it really was his phone before dropping his gaze and flicking through it.

'Make the call on loudspeaker,' she ordered. 'And just so you know, if it's not here by the time the sun comes up, I will update my blog and tell the world every nasty, vindictive thing you've done to me, you cruel, selfish *bastard.*'

Even though they both knew she could understand little of what was said, he did as she commanded, speaking in clipped tones to the voice groggy from sleep on the other end of the call. She felt not the slightest ounce of guilt. They'd stolen her boat. Stuff their sleep deprivation.

By the time the call was over, she'd managed to swallow her fury back into something that resembled calm. Giving another tight smile, she nodded. 'Thank you. Now, I'm going upstairs to get changed. Don't follow me.'

Keeping a tight hold of her grab-bag, she practically flew up the stairs and locked herself in her dressing room. She quickly changed into a non-constricting summer dress, wrenched the comb holding her chignon in place out of her hair, dumped her jewellery on her dresser and replaced the earrings with the studs from her parents, and put her old, flat sandals on.

The only falter in her movements came when she left the bedroom and reached the nursery. She reached for the door handle but then backed away before she could open it.

She wouldn't put herself through the pain of entering the room still waiting for the child who would never live in it. Not again.

But she would sit with Sophia under the

peach tree until the sun came up. Tell her everything would be okay. Tell her Mummy would be back to see her soon.

The front door was locked.

Keren punched in the code to override it. Nothing happened. Yannis must have changed it.

Fury filling her, she kicked it.

'Every door and window in the villa is locked. I'll deactivate the system after we've spoken.'

She whipped round and found Yannis at the threshold of the main living room. He'd removed his jacket and bow tie and undone the top couple of buttons of his shirt. His hair was sticking up in all directions. He carried a glass of what looked like bourbon.

Using all her might to harden her heart, she gazed at him coldly. 'I have nothing to say to you.'

'That's your prerogative but there's much I have to say to you.'

'I don't want to hear it.'

He shrugged. 'Again, your prerogative, but I *will* have my say. Sunrise isn't for another three hours. Block your ears until then if you must.'

The steel glimmering in his eyes told her clearly that he meant every word.

Fine. If he wanted to *have his say*, then fine. The sooner he'd said it, the sooner she could escape from this hellhole and its lying gaoler.

At the far end of the main living room was the bar. Keeping a tight hold of her grab-bag, Keren followed Yannis to it.

He clapped the lights on. 'What do you want to drink?'

'Nothing. I'll be sailing my boat in a few hours.'

His gaze clashed briefly with hers before he slipped behind the bar and pulled out a fresh bottle of bourbon and a bottle of cola. He pushed the cola and a glass to her.

The bar had sunken seats set around a range of tables. They were wonderfully cosy and just to look at them and remember just how cosy they'd got on them had Keren hoisting herself onto a bar stool. She hugged the grab-bag to her belly as if it were an amulet that could protect her.

Too late for protection.

She'd known when she sailed into Agon's waters that there was pain ahead, but she'd never dreamed she'd be ripping open a wound that had barely healed. And it was all her own fault. Yannis had shown his true colours in the eighteen months since she'd left him, and she'd swept all that aside and for what? Because he'd made love to her with the same passion that had first cemented their hearts together? Because she hadn't been strong enough to stop the grain of love from blooming back to life?

Because being with Yannis made her feel complete?

She'd swept aside, too, the simple fact that he'd fallen out of love with her. There had been no grain of love for her left in his heart.

He'd played her like a violin and her broken strings had fused back together and let him.

And now she must keep calm, hold firm and let him speak his lies. She would watch his mouth but not let his words penetrate. If, after he'd spoken his lies, he still refused to let her go, she would smash a window. She'd smash all the villa's windows if she had to.

He strode back to her side of the bar. Rather than take a seat, he stood close to her with his back against the bar and folded the arm not holding his drink around his waist.

He stared at her. Keren stared back stonily but refused to allow her eyes to focus. She couldn't. Gazing too deeply into his beautiful, masculine face made her weak. She needed to be strong.

'It is true,' he said quietly. 'My father and

brother did give me an ultimatum. There were many factors behind it.'

Startled that he'd started with a truth, Keren felt her stony features crumple and strove valiantly to pull them back into position. 'I'm sure. Must get the Filipidis production line going again.'

He flinched but didn't drop his stare. 'That was never a factor.'

She shrugged.

'It wasn't.'

'It really doesn't matter what the factors were. I should have known better. Why would the man who'd spent eighteen months acting so vindictively suddenly change his tune? As if you wanted me back.' She gave a small, sour laugh. 'At first I thought it was just more vindictiveness, then I assumed it was your pride talking—you not wanting to be the first Filipidis to divorce. About the only thing I didn't think of was pressure from your family and an ultimatum.'

'Their ultimatum wasn't the reason…' He took a deep breath and rubbed at his hair. It hurt her heart to see it stick up even more. 'Keren, I never wanted you to go in the first place.'

She dragged her gaze away from him. 'Well, we both know that's a lie.'

'You leaving… *Theos*, that was the last thing I wanted.'

'Could have fooled me from the way you threw my suitcases in the back of the taxi—'

'We've already been through this, and for someone who said they had nothing to say, you're not doing a very good job of letting me speak.'

'I just struggle listening to lies.'

'Or are you afraid of what I want to talk about?' he challenged.

The crawling ants returned to her skin with a vengeance.

'You researched divorce on your laptop,' she blurted out. At the naked shock on his face, she swallowed before adding, 'I looked in your laptop's search history.'

Silence surrounded them as if a vacuum had sucked out all the sound.

Something dark flashed over Yannis's face before he bowed his head and sighed heavily. 'You saw that?'

'Yes.'

'Why didn't you tell me?'

'I shouldn't have been looking, should I? You'd got all possessive about your laptop and kept closing the lid when I walked in on you with it. It was obvious you were hiding something.'

'That is not an answer.' His chest rose slowly. 'You should have confronted me. I would have confronted you if the roles had been reversed. And why didn't you mention it yesterday?'

Because she *couldn't*.

Because she'd been too scared, even when Yannis had locked her in the dressing room and she'd still believed she hated him, scared of hearing in his own words all the reasons he hated her enough to wish for a divorce. Knowing he wanted her out of his life…

That had been soul destroying.

'What would have been the point?' she asked bitterly. 'We both knew we were over and then a few days later you took Marla to that thing at the palace to spite me and humiliate me.'

His eyes closed and his chest rose again. 'It was to make you jealous.'

'What?'

'Taking Marla to the palace function. I was trying to get a reaction out of you.' He kneaded his fingers into his skull and shook his head. 'An idea that backfired spectacularly.' His eyes landed back on her. 'God forgive me. I wasn't thinking straight. I knew I was losing you.'

Keren felt suddenly winded. Her next, 'What?' was barely audible.

'I was losing you. I could feel it. It was my last roll of the dice to bring you back to me.'

She hugged her grab-bag even tighter to her bruised chest. The ants were biting into her skin, ravenous in their destruction. 'That's not true,' she whispered. 'You're the one who pulled away from me. You stopped loving me—'

'Never—'

'You turned your back on me every single night!' She could do nothing to stop the rise in her voice. 'You never touched me. I went from your lover to your possession. You wanted to control me—you admitted that only the other day!—and yet you hated me doing anything without you or without your permission!'

'For God's sake, Keren, why the hell do you think I behaved like that?' His own voice had risen in volume too. 'I was terrified.'

'Of *what*?'

'Everything!' he bellowed. Then he stilled, closed his eyes and exhaled slowly before focusing his stare back on her. 'I see it all so clearly now but when we were living it, it felt like this unstoppable force, a tsunami crashing on us and sweeping you away from me. I

didn't know how to reach you any more. You were slipping away from me and the harder I tried to pull you back, the harder you fought me. I didn't handle it well, I see that now, but I would not wish to live that time again so I could do things differently because I never want to live those days again and I would rather die than make you live a second of it. We both went to hell…'

The iced needles primed themselves against her heart. She could see where this was heading.

'Don't go there.' Her warning came out as a whimper.

He drank some of his bourbon and breathed in deeply. 'I *will* go there, *glyko mou*, because we have tiptoed around it too many times and destroyed our marriage because of it. Don't you remember how things were between us? How much we loved each other? Our marriage was working. *We* were working. From the day we met we fit together. You and me. But then we lost…'

She covered her ears and shook her head violently. 'Please. Yannis. Don't.'

But he removed her trembling hands and clasped them tightly in his.

His gaze bore into her, compassion mingled with the determination.

'We lost Sophia,' he continued. 'We lost her. Our baby died. And you broke.'

She shook her head. The back of her eyes were burning.

'You broke, Keren. And, God forgive me, I didn't know how to fix you.'

CHAPTER TWELVE

KEREN COULD FEEL the bruise of her rapid, icy heartbeats against her ribs and hear its staccato in her ear. Could feel the blood pumping through her body and gushing through the wail of the banshee locked in her head screaming its agony. A waterfall of hot, stinging tears poured down her face.

Yannis released her hands and palmed her sodden, trembling cheeks, catching and brushing the tears away with his thumb.

'I'm sorry for failing you,' he said hoarsely. 'All my life, the world has fallen on a plate for me. Bad things happen to other people. I wasn't equipped to deal with it, and I wasn't equipped to deal with a broken wife. You turned in on yourself. You hardly ate, you hardly spoke… Everyone said I had to give you time and space, and God knows I tried…'

'I never wanted space from *you*.' Her words choked their way out of her.

'But I didn't *know* that.'

She grabbed his shirt, making a fist of the cotton, and swallowed the worst of the tears away. 'You pushed me away.'

Sorrow etched his face. 'I'm sorry, *glyko mou*.'

'You stopped wanting me.'

'Yes.'

The brutality of his answer made her flinch.

She let go of his shirt, would have pushed him away if he hadn't moved his hands from her face into the tresses of her hair. 'I never stopped loving you,' he said. 'Never. But I couldn't make love to you. Those functions stopped working in me. All I could see was your face when you came round from the anaesthetic and I had to tell you we'd lost her.'

Nausea rolled violently and the iced needles plunged even deeper into Keren's heart as the most traumatic moment of her life echoed back through her, but she didn't pull her gaze from him because now all *she* could see for was the agony on Yannis's face when he'd broken the news to her.

'You broke too,' she whispered, voicing the realisation as it hit her.

'No.'

'You *did*.' She made another fist with

his shirt, remembering the giant sobs that had wracked his body when the nurse had brought Sophia to them and he'd cradled her lifeless but perfect form in his arms.

She'd been swaddled in a pink blanket, Keren remembered. She'd been so tiny and precious. Like a little doll.

Keren had stayed in her hospital bed for a week. Yannis had returned to an empty home.

The silence must have been deafening for him. Torturous.

And then she'd come home the day before the funeral and it had been like she'd been submerged in dark, murky water, too blinded by the darkness to see that Yannis was drowning too.

'Everything was put on your shoulders,' she remembered, her voice cracking. 'My care, the funeral...' She shook her head against the grief swelling back up. She needed to fight her way through it before it consumed her and doused the trail of her thoughts. 'You even chose the outfit we buried her in.'

Even the peach tree had been his idea. When they'd left the villa to choose it, it was the first time she'd left their home since the funeral.

'You were dealing with your own grief

and carrying the burden of a wife who was practically catatonic. That would have broken anyone.'

Yannis's jaw tightened before his beautiful face twisted and he shuddered. An animalistic howl ripped from his throat and he pulled her to him, crushing her tightly.

Keren held him just as tightly.

Her heart breaking at his pain, she clasped the back of his cradled head, wishing with all her heart that they'd done this two years ago.

Eventually, the tremors subsided and Yannis gently pulled out of the embrace. Cupping her cheeks in his hands, he gazed at her with damp eyes.

'Losing Sophia…' He swallowed. 'That was a pain I didn't know existed.' The pulses in his jaw throbbed. 'Not until they told me to prepare myself for losing you too. Keren… that would have killed me.'

The ice in her heart raced through to her veins at the starkness in his stare.

'But somehow you pulled through, and I was able to bring you home and you began to heal, but the healing was only physical. When you looked at me…' He swallowed again. 'Keren, there was nothing there. Nothing at all. And *Theos*, you were so fragile. It was like you were made of porcelain and all it needed was one little knock for you to shatter to pieces. I was terrified of being the one to inflict that knock on you. That's why I couldn't make love to you, even once you had healed, and I think it's why those functions stopped working in me—how could I make love to a woman made of porcelain without breaking her?'

Her stomach cramped violently to imagine his suffering.

Yannis had been locked in hell as much as she had.

She gently tugged his hands off her before asking in a small voice, 'Is that why you ended up turning to Marla?'

His face twisted again. 'I never turned to Marla or anyone. You have to believe that.'

'But you were with her all the time.'

He tipped his head back and sighed deeply. 'After we lost Sophia, Andreas ran the business single-handed for months. He worked himself into the ground. I owed him time off but by then I knew our marriage was in serious trouble. I didn't dare leave you for the time the business needed. Marla knows virtually everything about the business and was willing to step up to ease the workload for me until Andreas came back and we could put things back on a normal footing. It was just work. I swear.'

'But you took her to the palace function. How did you think making me jealous was going to repair things between us?'

'But that's just it—I wasn't thinking. By that stage, I was desperate and, God forgive me for this, I was starting to hate you. You'd pulled yourself out of your shell and everyone agreed you were better, but you *weren't* better.' His face tightened into a grimace. 'Not better with me. I'd always thought your father's error with your name had been a form of divine inspiration because the meaning of your name was the most apt of anyone I'd ever met. You were a ray of light that made my world a brighter, happier place from the day we met. You'd pulled yourself out of the darkness but the light that had always shone in you had gone and I couldn't read you any more, and that frightened me more than when you were lost in the darkness. That's why I got so angry when you announced you were going off to Morocco—it wasn't anger, it was fear.'

'What were you scared of?'

The distortion of his features at this question frightened her.

'Don't you understand?' he rasped. 'You

almost *died*. I thought I was going to have to bury you with our daughter. I have never known terror like it...' He clasped at his head. 'I developed this deep-rooted fear that if I let you out of my sight then something bad would happen to you. I couldn't bear to be parted from you and I *hated* the thought of you working and travelling anywhere without me there to keep you safe, but I didn't know how to reach you or talk to you and so I became more possessive and controlling. Every time I left the villa I was afraid I'd come home and find you gone. I even suggested having another baby, which is the most crass thing I could have asked of you. *Theos*, we hadn't made love in months and months. I could have made love to you, my desire had retuned, but I didn't know how to speak to you about it. To just try and make love...' He shook his head again. 'A wall had built between us and I didn't know how to break it. We hadn't really spoken either, had we, not properly, not unless you count shouting at each other as speaking. But I got it in my head that a baby would fix things, and you just looked at me like I was something dirty you'd trodden in and I knew...'

'Knew what?' she whispered when his words faltered.

His throat moved a number of times. He grabbed at his hair. 'That you were going to leave me. That's why I was looking on divorce sites. It wasn't for me. I was looking at how I could stop *you* from divorcing *me*.'

Her limbs weak, her heart ragged, Keren took his half-filled glass of bourbon off the bar and drank it in one swallow. Closing her eyes, she welcomed the burn of the liquid down her throat and the numbing of the pain engulfing her. 'I'm sorry for my part in everything too,' she whispered.

'You have nothing to be sorry for.'

'Yes, I do. I…' She swallowed. 'I…'

'What?' he asked gently.

Unable to get the words out, she brushed a tear away and swallowed as hard as she could. 'We didn't just lose our baby, did we? We lost *us*.'

'But you've found yourself again and now we can find us again. Look at how good things were for us these last few days. We're almost there. We can repair it. I know we can.'

Oh, his words hurt so much. Too much. 'It's too late.'

'No.'

'Yes. It's all gone too far. If you wanted me back because you still have feelings for me then I might have been able to forgive your despicable behaviour to me since I left and given us one more chance but not now. You've lied to me, over and over…'

'I have not.'

'You've used me, and dragging me down memory lane doesn't change that because for all that you said you were looking for divorce sites to stop me leaving you, that doesn't change the fact that the day I left, you *hated* me.' Her voice was rising again. She could do nothing to stop it. 'You threw my cases in the back of that taxi and called me a selfish cow and then you spent eighteen months systematically doing your best to impoverish me and I always knew why—you wanted me destitute so I would come crawling back, just as you predicted, and then you could have the satisfaction of being the one to kick me out and end our marriage and your pathetic pride would—'

'Yes! I hated you!'

Yannis's fury stopped her in her tracks.

'I hated that you were giving up on us without a fight, just like you're doing now, and I hated that there was nothing I could do or say to stop you, but I have never stopped loving you and God knows you've given me enough ammunition to kill my love.'

'What, wanting to start my blog up again?'

'Forget that damned blog! I'm talking about how you abandoned me and then cut me out of your life as if I'd never meant anything to you.'

'I didn't abandon you!' she cried. 'I left you.'

'It's the same thing!' he roared. 'Do you have *any* idea what it was like knowing the woman I loved was out there somewhere but not knowing where? I was going out of my mind! The first I knew you were even alive was when I received the divorce papers! I messed you around with the settlement, not because I wanted to impoverish you but because I was so damn desperate to see you. I wanted to make you angry enough to come home and confront me because I knew that if I could get you alone, we could sort things out, but you just went along with it and continued to ignore me.'

'I never cared about the settlement,' she whispered. 'I just wanted us over with.'

'You think I didn't know that? You wanted to forget I'd ever existed and that destroyed me, but I couldn't give up. And then I got an alert that your blog was active again.'

She blinked in shock.

'Does the username WannabeWanderer mean anything to you?'

All the air left her lungs.

WannabeWanderer was one of her regular blog followers, someone who commented on every post and asked a ton of questions about her life at sea.

'That was *you*?'

'Yes. *Theos*, the blog I'd grown to hate became my lifeline. I could read your words and know you were alive and safe. I could ask you questions and you would answer them—your words, your real words, directed to me. I would study the pictures and videos you posted, and I began to see you emerge. The real you. The Keren I first fell in love with. But you were too safety-conscious to post your exact location and I could never find you.'

'You tried to track me down?'

'I have spent more time on *The Amphitrite* than anywhere else this last year. But I never found you.' He shook his head with a grim smile. 'I had it all planned. How I would act when I found you. Pretend that it was coincidence. Resist from abducting you and locking you in a cabin until you agreed to come home.'

The snigger flew from her lips before she even knew it had formed.

Their eyes met. Locked.

Keren sighed. And Yannis sighed too.

When he opened his mouth to speak again, there was no more anger in his voice. Just sadness. 'I don't think I slept properly in all the time you were gone. I had nightmares about you getting into trouble on the open sea and no one being close enough to save you. I would charge to your rescue but my dreams were like my life—I could never find you.

'I neglected the business. I neglected my family. I neglected my duties. I hated the world. I picked fault in everyone and everything. Most of my household staff quit—that's why there are so many unfamiliar faces here. If not for Andreas working in the background soothing egos, we would have lost half the staff who work for the business. The Legarde contract…that's not the only mess I made. It was much worse than me just taking my eye off the ball. I lost all interest in the ball. That's what the meeting with Andreas and my father was about. They didn't really have a choice. I was screwing up too much. The only ultimatum was that I needed to pull myself together or they would force me off the board. You were mentioned only because they knew that your leaving was the root cause of it all. They gave me some home truths too, about the man I was turning into and asked me to consider why the hell you would want to come back to that man. They made me see I was screwing everything up for everyone, and they were right. I look back at the person I became and I feel shame.'

'Pavlos said they were pressurising you about producing an heir.'

His laughter was cynical. 'They were pressuring Andreas and Pavlos, sure. Lots of hints. Some subtle. Most not. The only time they ever spoke about heirs to me was when they'd had too much to drink, patronising rubbish about how you and I could try again when I got you back. It was meant to be comforting. Supportive. You know what they're like.'

Keren closed her eyes.

Yes. She did. They never meant to be cruel. Like when Nina had given her the business card of her personal shopper—she'd thought she was doing a kind deed to her future daughter-in-law. Image was important to the Filipidises, but not as important as the business itself, and that came second in the pecking order to family.

'I knew that this weekend had to be it for me.'

She opened her eyes.

'I knew you would come and see Sophia for her birthday.' A sad smile played on his lips. 'All the time I've been searching for you… Keeping my promise to let you visit her undisturbed is the hardest promise I've ever had to keep. My staff always notified me when you were here, but I kept the promise and always waited until you sailed away before setting off after you.' His smile widened. 'You always disappeared. I thought your boat must be painted chameleon colours.'

She smiled back. 'I told you—small boats can access coves and things that bigger boats can't.'

'I'm still not selling *The Amphitrite* for something smaller than my dressing room.' The brief flare of amusement died. His throat moved again, and he bowed his head before meeting her stare. 'I knew that, this weekend, I had to break that promise. It's the only promise in my life I've broken. I knew this had to be my last attempt to win you back and that if I failed, it was time for me to let you go. And now that I have failed, I will keep my word.'

Unsure what he meant, she watched him swipe his phone.

His features tightened briefly before his shoulders rose. 'As I thought. Your boat has been returned.' He poured himself a large measure of the bourbon, drank it in one, wiped his mouth with the back of his hand then visibly braced himself. 'It is time for you to leave.'

She just stared at him, hardly able to breathe.

He bowed his head over his phone again. 'Give me one minute.'

'Yannis?'

He didn't look up. 'Please, *glyko mou*. One minute…'

Her throat stayed closed until he lifted his head and said, 'Done.'

The expression in his eyes was one she hadn't seen before. It frightened her.

'I have deactivated the locks,' he explained evenly. 'You are free to leave. I give you my word I will not follow you or try to find you. I have also transferred ten million euros into your account as part of the original settlement. I will transfer the remainder on Monday…'

Panic scratched at her throat. 'I don't want your money.'

He shrugged. 'I know you don't but it's yours. Buy another boat. Give it to charity. Do what you like with it. Give the divorce papers to your lawyer on Monday. It takes ten days for a judge here to stamp it and make it official, and then we will both be free.'

'Free?' she repeated dumbly. 'So that's it? You're letting me go?'

His lips curved in a smile so sad her heart heaved. 'What else can I do? You are mine and I am yours and I would never give up on you or give up on us, but I see now that it isn't about giving up. It's about what's best for you and best for me, and that means letting you go. There were times since you came back that I thought I was winning— that *we* were winning—but I have to accept that I'm beaten. You accepted what Pavlos told you without question because you want to go—'

'That's not how it was.'

'It is,' he stated firmly. 'You never wanted to come back. I forced this time on you. I knew from the day I met you that holding onto you would be an impossible task. I have to accept that your trust in me is destroyed and learn to live my life without you. It's not fair on either of us for me to try to fix something that's beyond repair. I will always love you, *glyko mou*, but it's time for us both to move on and put the past behind us.'

Still dumbfounded at the turn of events, Keren could only stare as Yannis headed off through to the entertainment room and pressed the button that opened the bifold wall-length door. Holding her grab-bag tightly, she followed him through it to the outdoor entertainment space.

On the horizon, the first peak of the sun cut through the darkness.

The outside lights in the distance came on. A figure emerged, walking towards them.

'That will be Niki with your boat keys,' Yannis said quietly.

The keys were handed to her in silence. She slipped them in her pocket. They were weightier than she remembered.

Then Niki disappeared.

'This is where I bid you farewell,' Yannis said in a lighter voice. 'I will leave you to say goodbye to Sophia. I wish you safe travels.'

'Thank you,' she croaked. Everything had turned on its head so rapidly she was struggling to make her voice work as much as she was struggling to make her brain work. 'Keep yourself safe too.'

'Always.'

They stared at each other for a long, drawn-out moment before Yannis brushed a gentle thumb over her cheek. 'Goodbye, *glyko mou*.'

'Goodbye, Yannis.'

He bowed his head one last time and turned, his long legs taking him steadily back to the villa.

He didn't look back.

CHAPTER THIRTEEN

THE ENGINE TURNED at the first attempt.

Keren clasped hold of the tiller. She had to hold it firmly. Her hand was shaking.

The birds were out in force that early morning, flying above her, squawking and singing, drowning out the sound of her heartbeat which had been banging like a drum in her ear since Yannis had walked away.

She set sail through the still, clear waters.

Where should she go first? Crete? Sicily? She would make it out of Agon waters and then decide. The whole world was her oyster.

A small breeze whipped her hair into her face. She pulled it back and wound it into a practised knot.

It was natural that she should feel battered and bruised, she told herself. It had been an emotional night. And she hadn't had any sleep. That probably explained why she felt so sick too. Bad sick. Not good sick.

She would sail for Crete, she decided. It wouldn't take her long to get there. When she'd anchored or found a marina, she would go and find somewhere to have some breakfast. Food should quell the growing nausea.

An image of Yannis eating an omelette alone on the pool terrace and drinking gallons of coffee from his *briki* came into her mind. She banished it.

Yannis was her past. She was free of him.

He'd finally let her go.

She spotted a ferry, guessed that it, too, was headed to Crete. No doubt it was full of holiday makers. Couples. Families.

That was what she would do. Sail to England like she'd thought of doing earlier and visit her family. Tell them she loved them. She wished she could apologise for never being physically present with them but they wouldn't understand what she was apologising for. They'd always accepted their little cuckoo. If not for their love and support, Keren would never have been able to set out on her adventures when she'd been only eighteen. They'd known since she was twelve that she would flee their nest the moment that she could and had prepared accordingly. Their leaving present to her had been a laptop and five hundred pounds. Weekly emails and the occasional visit from her was enough for them. They only wanted her to be happy, however bemused they were by how she found that happiness.

She would stay for a few days with them and…

The Filipidises had accepted her as she was too. They'd had reservations about her being an outsider, but they'd done their best to accept her into their family. Despite their differences, they'd grown to love her and she'd grown to love them. They'd embraced the cuckoo in their nest just as her own family had done.

And Yannis…

Yannis had never needed to accept her because he'd always understood her. Always. Even in their darkest days when their world had been ripped apart, he'd understood her.

A rip tore through her heart, doubling her over at the pain it unleashed.

What was she *doing*?

Turning her back and sailing away from the one person in the world she'd found her home with? The man who loved her, truly loved her, with all his possessive need for her? The one man she'd found true happiness with?

Yannis had been nothing but constant and

what had she given him in return? She'd thrown his love back at him. Fear had caused that. Terror of loving him again and watching his love for her die all over again. The loss of his love on the heels of losing their daughter had been too much and she'd shut down, and she'd shut down her love and all other feelings with it.

But his love had never died. Never. She'd just been too heartsick with grief to recognise it, too blinded by her own pain to see his fear and suffering.

Her love had never died either. Yannis had awoken it again and now it blazed in her heart as brightly as the sun shining above her. He'd done many things wrong—they both had—but he'd been right about so many other things. He'd always known that if he could get her back in their home and keep her there long enough, then her love for him would bloom back to summer, because their love was everything and always had been.

And she'd known it too.

She could have left at any time. Yannis had signed the divorce papers. He'd let her keep them. If she'd been really, truly determined to leave, she would have walked out with them all the way to her lawyer and then the British Embassy. He wouldn't have stopped her.

But she hadn't. She hadn't because deep in her heart, she'd wanted to stay. She'd just been too frightened to admit it. Too frightened of opening herself to more pain.

Dear heavens, what had she *done*?

Grasping tightly to the tiller and grasping tightly to her emotions, she turned the boat around.

Agon appeared in the distance. The first tears broke through. There was nothing she could do about them or the acute pain punching through her with every beat of her heart.

Ignoring the jetty, she sailed as close to the beach as she could before the boat grounded and she jumped into the water and swam harder than she'd ever swum before. Salt water dripping off her from head to toe, uncaring that she'd lost her sandals, she ran over the sand and then up the steps. Not pausing when she reached the top, she raced to the olive grove and pulled apart the mound of rocks she'd hidden the plastic food bag under.

And then she ran to the villa, skidding to a stop when she reached the pool area.

Where was Yannis?

He must know she was here. His security team would have told him the second she sailed into his waters.

And as she realised that, realised that he

must know she was there and that his absence could only mean that he'd finally given up on her, another, even bigger wrench ripped through her heart, dropping Keren to her knees with a keening wail.

It was too late. *She* was too late.

The child she'd carried with such love for eight months, celebrating each and every movement that had rippled through her belly, had died. It was too late to save her. She was gone.

And it was too late to save her marriage. That was gone too.

The banshee that had lived in her head for so long finally found its way free and Keren's wail became a scream that ripped out from deep inside her as the loss of those she'd loved with every fibre of her being finally smashed into her and through her in one huge tsunami of grief.

Burying her face in her knees and pounding at the ground beneath her, Keren screamed until she was hoarse. And then she wept. She wept for her child. She wept for her husband. She wept for the destruction of the dreams they'd held so dear and a love that had been so strong.

All gone. All gone.

A pair of hands touched her shoulders and

then she was being hauled onto the lap of the man she loved and rocked and held so tightly that her tears soaked into his shirt.

Only when she had a degree of control over the tears did she lift her head and put her hands to his cheeks to face him. Seeing the rawness of his eyes sliced her with fresh pain. *She* had caused that.

'Oh, Yannis,' she choked. 'I thought I was too late.'

'Never. I was running.'

'Running?'

'I thought I'd lost you for good. I needed to do…*something*. The staff spotted you and sent out the search for me. I got to you as fast as I could.'

'I'm so, so sorry. I did abandon you. I *did*. I truly thought you didn't love me any more and I just couldn't bear it.'

'Hush,' he whispered, pulling her back to him and pressing his mouth into her hair. 'It's okay, *glyko mou*. It's okay.'

'No. It isn't. I need to explain… You know what you said about an unstoppable force crashing in on us and sweeping me away from you? Well, that's how it felt for me too, but it was like you were fading away from me and no matter how hard I stretched my arms, I couldn't reach you to touch you.'

He tightened his hold around her. 'It's okay, *glyko mou*. I understand.'

'You've always understood me.' She squeezed her eyes shut against more tears. 'I can't tell you how sorry I am that I stopped trying to understand you and that I pushed you away. The whole world…everything was so *dark*, but when I found my way out everything had changed, like the sparkle had gone out of the world. And I found that I hated you.'

She felt him flinch.

Lifting her face to look at his, she stroked her fingers across his cheeks. 'I did. I hated you for not wanting to make love to me. I hated you for having to work. I hated that you didn't want me to work. I hated you for suffocating me but then I hated you for giving anyone else any kind of attention. I was so *angry*, and so wrapped up in my fears and pain, that I never appreciated how scared you were too.'

'My fears were all wrapped up in us and I know now that I made things worse for both of us.'

'We both did.'

'Yes. And that is why I now think that you leaving was for the best.'

'How?' She disentangled herself so she

could straighten and look at him properly, utterly bewildered that he would say such a thing.

'You couldn't heal here,' he answered simply. 'That's all you needed. To heal. And you couldn't heal here with me... You cried in your sleep nearly every single night.'

That bewildered her even more. 'I did?'

His face spasmed and he said hoarsely, 'I would stroke your hair to calm you—it's the only time I dared touch you. Then in the morning you would wake, and I knew you didn't remember but I couldn't talk to you about it. I didn't dare. But if I hadn't made you hate me by acting like such a possessive fool, you would have confided your feelings and fears in me.'

'And if I hadn't got lost in the darkness I would have reached harder for you before you were frightened into acting like such a possessive fool.'

The whisper of a smile played on his lips but his eyes were full of sorrow. 'Keren, you were suffering from depression.'

'And you weren't?'

'I didn't carry our baby inside me for eight months.'

'But you loved her the same as I did. You had the same hopes and dreams as I did.'

He cupped her cheeks tightly and stared at her as if he were trying to burrow into her head and imprint his thoughts into it. 'It wasn't the same for me. I always knew that. And it tears my soul to know I couldn't be the rock you needed to lean on to get you through it, but I swear on our daughter's soul that I will never turn away from you again.'

'I will never turn from you either,' she swore. 'Never.'

'If you stay, I swear that I will love and cherish you until my dying day. If bad days come for us again then we will face them together.'

Her chest filled with an emotion so sweet she could almost taste it.

She pressed her nose to his. 'There has not been a minute of my life since I left you when I haven't felt you with me. You are everything to me. My whole world. I love you, Yannis.'

A spasm of emotions flittered over his face before his features relaxed and the darkness in his eyes lifted. 'And I love you. More than anything.'

Yannis's kiss contained such love and tenderness that if she'd had any lingering doubts they would have been expelled. But she didn't. The feeling of rightness was too strong.

Palming his cheek, she gazed into his eyes again and whispered, 'What do you think about us going to her nursery and deciding what we're going to do with it?'

He breathed in deeply. 'You are ready?'

'If you're with me.'

'I will always be with you.'

'I know.' She smiled. 'But before we do anything else, I have something for you.'

His brow furrowed in question.

She pulled the plastic food bag out of her pocket and handed it to him.

He stared at it blankly before understanding had him drop it as if it were laced with poison.

'Shred it,' she told him.

'Shred it then burn it?'

'Then throw the ashes into the sea.'

Laughing, he kissed her again.

Wrapping her arms tightly around him, melting into the heat of his mouth, the feeling of rightness grew even stronger.

The cuckoo had found her way home. Her home was wherever Yannis was.

EPILOGUE

THE PHOTOGRAPHER'S SMILE was starting to look a bit forced, Keren noted. His entreaties for everyone to hold a pose and smile for him were starting to sound a bit clipped, and she tried not to laugh when she caught Yannis's eye and saw that he'd noticed too.

'Phoebe, get back here!' she called when their youngest daughter once again escaped her grandfather's clutches, this time to chase a butterfly.

Keren let go of Yannis's hand and, laughing, hair streaming behind her, ran after their wilful three-year-old and scooped her up.

As she marched a frantically wriggling Phoebe back to Aristidis, she noticed six-year-old Ioanna, her hand clasped in Andreas's, shake her head at her uncle over her little sister's antics. Just as Keren had always baffled her family, Phoebe baffled Ioanna. Her daughters came from opposite ends of the personality spectrum. Ioanna was bookish and already developing a love for art and history. Phoebe was away with the fairies. Keren loved them both so much her heart hurt.

Realising that Phoebe was building up a head of steam for a full-blown temper tantrum, which would no doubt cause the harassed photographer to have his own full-blown temper tantrum, Keren whispered, 'How would you like to go fishing with me tomorrow?'

What she called fishing actually meant taking small fishing nets to the rock pools at the cove on the opposite side of the jetty, scooping up the crabs and tiny fish caught in them, putting them into seawater-filled buckets and then carefully putting them back out to sea. Phoebe was fascinated with sea life and, having recently watched a cartoon film about a mermaid, declared that she was one too.

Phoebe stopped wriggling and considered the question. Then she cupped her plump hand to Keren's ear and whispered back, 'Nanny Nina come too?'

Keren sniggered. Nina had recently accompanied them on one of their fishing expeditions. Phoebe had held a crab in her hand and proudly lifted it up to Nina's horrified face.

'We can ask,' she told her, 'but only if you behave yourself.'

She was rewarded with a mischievous giggle.

Handing a now-docile Phoebe back to Aristidis, Keren hurried back to Yannis's side. Grinning at each other, their hands clasped together and their fingers interlinked.

With the troublemaker now on her best behaviour, the photographer quickly barked fresh orders and the entire Filipidis clan retook their original positions in front of the peach tree and, on his order, smiled widely.

Click, click, click.

Keren and Yannis's tenth wedding anniversary portrait was immortalised.

Within an hour, just as the sun was starting to set, the best photos of this day of celebration landed in Yannis's in-box. He called everyone over and opened his laptop at the table by the pool and connected it to the projector he'd had set up in anticipation.

Keren sat herself on his left lap to watch, Ioanna on his right, cuddling in to Keren, her soft dark curls tickling Keren's neck and chin. Yannis held them both tightly. He always held them tightly.

Phoebe had fallen asleep under a table.

One by one, the photos flashed before them. The photographer had captured all the best moments of the day, from her supposedly gluten-free mother-in-law stuffing her face with a piece of anniversary cake, to Pavlos being pushed into the pool by the kids, to Keren and Yannis stealing one of a hundred kisses stolen that day. But it was the family portrait beneath the peach tree that Keren and, she knew, Yannis were most looking forward to seeing. These were the photos that included Sophia, their eldest child. Her peach tree had grown so huge and sprawling that her branches made a canopy over the entire family.

Their daughter was lost to them from life but not from their memories or their hearts. Her tree made her at one with them, something that brought them both great comfort.

There were a dozen pictures of the whole family under Sophia's tree, and as the images on the projector changed, Keren reflected on what a lucky cuckoo she was. She had a husband who worshipped and cherished her, who took pride in everything she did and whom she was as madly in love with as she'd been the day she married him. She had two clever, inquisitive, beautiful daughters, a loving family at home in England and a loving set of in-laws here at home in Agon.

Her heart swollen with happiness and love, she lifted Yannis's hand to her mouth and kissed it. He dropped a kiss into the top of her head.

Just as she was thinking, again, that she was a very lucky cuckoo indeed, the sniggers started.

The very last picture on the digital album being projected before them had the entire Filipidis clan: Keren and Yannis, their children, Yannis's brother and brother-in-law, parents, grandparents, aunts, uncles, cousins and cousins' children, all smiling in perfect harmony. All except for Phoebe, who had her tongue out and was making devil horns above her oblivious grandfather's head.

'That one is going to be trouble,' Nina observed in an undertone from behind them.

Yannis caught Keren's eye, grinned and winked. 'I know,' he said. 'She's just like her mother.'

* * * * *

If you got lost in the drama of
Stranded with Her Greek Husband
*you're sure to love these other stories
by Michelle Smart!*

The Billionaire's Cinderella Contract
The Cost of Claiming His Heir
The Forbidden Innocent's Bodyguard
The Secret Behind the Greek's Return
Unwrapped by Her Italian Boss

Available now!